Leïla Marouane was born in Algeria in 1960. She has worked as a journalist in Algiers, Berlin, Zurich and Paris. Her first novel, *La Fille de la Casbah*, was published in Paris in 1996. *The Abductor* is her second novel and the first to be published in English. She now divides her time between Paris and Zurich.

Felicity McNab was educated at Trinity College, Dublin. She is a freelance translator and musicologist and lives in Ireland.

the abductor

leïla marouane

Translated by Felicity McNab

Ω

Quartet Books

This translation is dedicated to Brian

First published in Great Britain by Quartet Books Limited in 2000
A member of the Namara Group
27 Goodge Street
London W1P 2LD

Originally published in French under the title *Le Ravisseur*

A catalogue record for this book is available from the
British Library

ISBN 0 7043 8142 7

Phototypeset by FiSH Books, London
Printed and bound in Great Britain by Cox & Wyman, Reading, Berks

To my mother and father. Always.
For Aicha–Nina and little Abla

The flags are at half-mast and the orchestra is
counting its cripples.
Oliver Py, *The Face of Orpheus*

Leïla Marouane was born in Algeria in 1960. She has worked as a journalist in Algiers, Berlin, Zurich and Paris. Her first novel, *La Fille de la Casbah*, was published in Paris in 1996. *The Abductor* is her second novel and the first to be published in English. She now divides her time between Paris and Zurich.

Felicity McNab was educated at Trinity College, Dublin. She is a freelance translator and musicologist and lives in Ireland.

part one

1

My father lay helpless on the sofa while my mother was being joined to Youssef Allouchi in lawful wedlock.

My mother's husband lived in the little house opposite our own. We could see straight into his garden which filled our balconies with its perfume, and neither water shortages nor drought got the better of his honoured blooms, every night that God gave, against the background of the songs of an unfailing nightingale.

In the past, long, long ago, when my parents wanted to go up country to the land of their birth, my brother brought home his friends, then charged them a fee for being allowed to look at what was then called the Garden of a Thousand Perfumes and Colours. Or something like that.

3

Youssef Allouchi was fifty-five years old and had never been married. In the neighbourhood it was said that he was possessed by a woman from another world, a jinnee, and the most malicious neighbours suspected he was sexually impotent. Whatever the reason for his celibacy, it had given my father sufficient excuse to arrange his engagement to my mother.

Youssef Allouchi was handsome – he had fair skin, gentle hands, as well as a young man's legs, and his eyes slanted upwards when he smiled. He also happened to be our most elegant and cultured neighbour by a long way. As a scribe, a poet and a bit of a philosopher, he spoke French as well as he spoke Arabic, and had possibly mastered other languages too.

When he was not in the square in front of the Town Hall, where he set up his desk, his typewriter and his pens, he could be seen in the local park, reading Racine, Al-Maari, or the Qur'an...If you happened to pass, he would read to you for a few minutes, in whichever language you chose. He used to say, so sensually that it sent shivers down your spine and turned your good clothes into rags, that it was food for your soul. The gossips saw this as the power of the woman from the other world.

Apart from his mother, who was Christian or maybe even Jewish – no one knew any more than that – who had been dead for over ten years now and whom he had held particularly dear, we knew of no other family, nor acquaintances who could have been described as friends. However, since the death of his mother, every three months, first thing in the morning, you would meet him on the station road, with his little black leather suitcase in one hand, his typewriter in the other, and a satchel stuffed with books under his arm.

He would reply to indiscreet questions impassively:
'Professional duties, you know...'

That was all we knew.

He would come back three or four weeks later, with a spring in his step, looking tanned, and with a smile that would put the brightest sun to shame. Where did he go? Who did he go to see? After definitively ruling out the possibility that it could be an assignation, we imagined that he indulged in the extravagances related to his eloquence and culture: making speeches, writing pamphlets, organizing meetings...Yes, maybe he was organizing a *coup d'état* that would soon make our district famous. Obviously, we were only joking; this was a way of teasing someone who was beyond our control just because he was different...Who, for heaven's sake, could claim at that time to be involved in the dim and tumultuous paths of a revolution? Or even insinuate that your neighbour was involved? And even if we only dropped hints about him, so near as he was but so far from our doors, these days the earth shook, trembled, was carved up and it swallowed up human beings under the approving eye of faceless men declaiming Texts which were known only to themselves. So we stopped making jokes of this kind, seeing that the escapades of our learned neighbour were no longer of interest to anyone.

My mother understood very soon that she could not escape my father's decision that she should marry again and was resigned to this, even going so far as to express a wish to be represented by him at the ceremony. This request was thrown out by our man of the law, as my father's role of legal guardian was null and void from that time onwards. But when she found out my father's choice, my mother sank into the depths of despair. Not that she attached any importance to Youssef Allouchi's virility, but the neighbours' tongues were already wagging.

2

On the eve of the ceremony, the Imam who acted as our advisor on religious matters came to find out whether all was going well with the engagement. My mother threw herself at his feet, kissed them and clasped them to her.

'If I absolutely must remarry, let it be with someone normal, and far, far away, let it not be in this neighbourhood,' she pleaded.

'As if it's up to her to choose herself a husband!' my father roared when the Imam told him about my mother's refusal.

'One doesn't renounce one's wife lightly, three times,' said the Imam in his clear voice.

'That can't be undone,' said my father contritely. 'Today we must get on with celebrating this wedding…'

'She has a right to object to it.'

'And who will marry her for me, except Youssef Allouchi?'

'God will provide,' said the Imam.

'So we agree, but if no one is found...'

'God would wish it so...'

'God has shown us Youssef Allouchi.'

'A marriage must be consummated,' the Imam let slip.

'Don't be a slanderer,' my father retorted, looking askance at the man. 'You're an Imam, after all...'

'You know very well what I mean,' the Imam whispered, blushing.

'Youssef Allouchi, who knows the Qur'an as well as you know it yourself, knows that a marriage must be consummated.'

'Why not wait a little while?'

'We can't wait anymore!' my father roared again.

He was breathing and sweating as if a sandstorm were blowing. 'We've been waiting now for three months,' he continued calmly. 'For three months the mother of my children hasn't been sleeping at home... if this repudiation isn't sorted out, what shall I do with the children? You know very well that I've got enough of them, and some are really young, the youngest – another little girl – is still a babe in arms... six girls... There are six girls under this roof who need their mother...'

He made himself giddy listing us all. Still, he remembered us, our ages, our shortcomings... and as with every family disaster, he began to describe our faults so fervently that we ended up being convinced of them.

'Samira, who's nineteen, is unpredictable, a runaway, a liar, as far as I remember she's a self-confessed trouble-maker. Oh, yes, she's aggressive! An aggressive girl who by herself can start off tribal disputes. And then Yasmina and Amina, who're both sixteen, which makes thirty-two, sticking to each other the whole blessed day, chattering sluts, dawdling at school, a waste of money, for the State and for myself... Anyway I wonder why they don't throw them out. They'll finish up as dressmakers. If they're lucky!'

He served tea to the Imam. The liquid spurted out and spilled on the table, he was shaking so much. So he decided not to fill his own glass and started again:

'Noria, the thirteen-year-old, who stumbles over her words and will spend her life stammering. Also, she walks in her sleep or sleeps while she walks, it doesn't matter which – she certainly doesn't function normally. How many times has she not been caught at the corner of the street? Fouzia, who's eleven or twelve, I'm not sure... When she was born, while she was letting out her first cries, my loveliest trawler caught fire, on a day when it was raining cats and dogs,' he went on. 'Even today, she's only got to open her mouth to make a disaster fall on our heads... Last time she was heard, my poor aunt, may God have mercy on her soul, burst her gall-bladder. Zanouba or Manouba, whoever, arrived recently, unexpectedly, born with the strength of a bear and, despite being very premature, already showed signs that were nothing to rejoice about. Only God knows what disastrous form she will grow out of her nappies into...Six daughters who couldn't boil an egg without their mother. Six daughters who'll have to be brought up, who'll never be real women, they'll be damaged goods! They'll have to be married off forcibly, with fisticuffs and a bagful of money. Mind you, the eldest is certainly unmarriageable.' He gave a long, meditative sigh. But he went on:

'Who'd want a daughter who's no longer a virgin? Don't look so amazed, Imam. In this district there are no impregnable secrets. It doesn't upset me any more – in fact nothing upsets me any more. I'm condemned to see and have this sham of a daughter under my roof until the end of my days. I couldn't get rid of her for a million dollars.'

My father's voice was loud and deep, his nose and his forehead shone like lumps of fat, and when he stopped talking, his mouth closed in a sad half-moon.

'If I don't take back my wife, do you think I could find another one to look after my menagerie?' he went on in a brusque, broken voice.

He was quiet for a moment. Then, lowering his voice:

'Moreover, it isn't just the girls. Even the eldest one, the boy, isn't worth tuppence. Instead of being interested in his studies, he's let his sideburns grow and has had the clever idea of getting married – and I've asked him why. He answered, "For the *sunna* of Allah and of his Prophet." At the age of twenty, Omar, my only son, is already a father... "For the *sunna* of Allah and of his Prophet, da dada, da dada," my father said, imitating my brother's voice.

Then in response to the Imam's frown and reproving look:

'I don't want to offend you, *sidi*, but sincerely and just between ourselves, getting married at this age, in an era where men and even women, are going to the moon, where Mars is a swimming pool... Do you see what I mean? In short, I had planned a future for him which wasn't that of young fatherhood...'

The Imam listened uncomplainingly, sometimes shaking his head from right to left, then from left to right, as if he was trying to find the relationship between my father's utterances and my mother's refusal.

And our superstitious father went on:

'If this child hadn't been born, I wouldn't have repudiated my wife...'

Then:

'As if I needed a grandson...'

The Imam nodded gently again, stroked his excuse for a moustache, coughed and said categorically:

'One cannot force a woman to marry a man she doesn't want.'

It took my father all of his strength to stand up.

'And who taught you these truths, Imam?'

His sudden use of the familiar form 'tu' did not

bode well. Imam though he was, the man who now shivered in his white *gandoora* could not escape the flood of insults and hurtful remarks that poured out of my father.

Just like his father before him, our own father was known for not treating anyone with kid gloves, and we didn't know anyone who had ever dared to stand up to him. It must be said that we, had the largest house in the district and the largest trawlers in the harbour. Also, even though generosity wasn't his strong point, my father respected the annual almsgiving to the letter. Every summer, as he had promised his father on his deathbed, he gave away one tenth of his income to be shared out among the disadvantaged members of the community. Then there was the building of the mosque, where our Imam preached, financed by our grandfather, in memory of his wife who had departed prematurely...

'It's in the Holy Book,' muttered the Imam.

My father went into battle again.

'I already do a lot for the Holy Book!' he exploded. 'Do you think I have leanings towards sinning? It's true, and it's well known, I have a weakness for red wine, that's my only enslavement, and God will be merciful to me. Don't you think so, Imam?'

The Imam was showing signs of fatigue. Without saying a word he took out his handkerchief and dabbed his forehead.

'Am I not in fact applying the laws of Allah? I could just as well have taken back the mother of my children without expending all this energy,' my father said, certain now that he had found the right justification for his decision. 'Nobody would have known that I had repudiated her – except her and me . . . and Allah. Isn't that true?'

The Imam agreed.

'Then no one will have any problem with her getting married again to Youssef Allouchi,' my father concluded. 'I have taken it upon myself to offer him her hand and if he has accepted, it's because of his generous heart.'

My father pursed his lips tightly and took a furtive look at the Imam. Strengthened by the feeling of victory that was enveloping him, he skilfully poured himself some tea and swallowed a mouthful. As if talking to himself, he said:

'She married me under duress. And she wasn't sixteen. That didn't stop us having the children you know and being together for more than twenty years.'

He stopped short, thunderstruck, his mouth half-open as if he wished this last sentence would vanish, carried away by the breeze. Sweat was running down his face, but he turned so pale it suddenly seemed to dry up. What if his wife, who in three seconds would become his ex-wife, went to live for the next twenty years under the roof of Youssef Allouchi? In other words, what would happen if, for one reason or another, our elegant neighbour did not repudiate my mother, as he had tacitly promised my father? As the Imam and the district were expecting? Some people congratulated themselves on the introduction of temporal marriage and its benefits, charitably thanking its promoters in our country and, of course, the Shiite, those Persians who were definitely more civilized than us rigid Sunnis with no imagination. Then there was the unspoken regret that Youssef Allouchi could not take advantage of it . . . But who was to know? Maybe, after all . . .

My father drank his tea in one gulp, put the glass down on the table, cut the air with his hand and vigorously shook his head, to get rid of this annoying idea: what mattered was to hold on to the reasons which had led him to set his sights on our distinguished neighbour. He peered at the Imam, called upon God's grace, recalled the urgency of my mother's remarriage, the three months required by convention coming to an end . . .

'And the divorce?' our legal man suddenly enquired.

My father gave a start.

'Isn't she divorced by saying so three times?'

'The civil divorce . . .'

'No need for that,' said my father, who had been caught on the hop. Then with a look and a stony face:

'All of that will remain between ourselves. It won't do us any good to get the courts mixed up in this story. I'm doing this for the kids, as I've already told you.'

'All the same, it's illegal,' muttered our religious adviser.

Our father swallowed.

'Isn't true marriage that which you bless?'

An echoing silence answered his question. It was as if the whole house held its breath, with its eyes wide open and a finger at its lips, waiting for the Imam to reject the fate that should join – in a brief and ephemeral manner – my mother and Youssef Allouchi.

Behind the curtain separating the living-room from the drawing-room, where my father and the Imam were installed, my mother was standing, without moving, like a Greek statue. She was weeping silently and was staring at the curtain as if her eyes could see through the opaque fabric. From time to time, she licked the tears that gathered on her full red upper lip. A faint premonition came over me and I stared hard at her. Should I console her or pretend to know nothing and get on with my own business, thus obeying my father, who had forbidden us from interfering? Should I laugh or cry over what was happening to my parents? Did such situations exist anywhere else? I would have given my life for it to be normal. But the gossip which had set the district rocking told me otherwise.

I sorted out my things unhurriedly, hoping that my mother would make a sign to me, would ask me for advice or to help her or just to hold her in my arms and weep with her. But that was a vain hope, as her tender impulses were directed solely towards the masculine gender. Having recently become a grandmother, and of a little boy, my mother longed for nothing more than the happiness of seeing many grandchildren born and growing up, and the tears flowing down her cheeks were definitely tears of shame.

I coughed to announce my presence. Once more, my mother licked her lips and her large eyes, made smaller by her tears, did not meet mine.

When I crossed the doorstep, my little sister, Zanouba or Manouba (it took us time to settle for Zanouba), started to wail in her cradle.

And my father shouted:

'Do you hear what I mean, Imam!'

And the Imam replied 'I shall celebrate this wedding on condition that everything is done according to the rules: witnesses, legal guardian, etcetera.'

And thus the Imam persuaded my mother, and my mother borrowed a wedding veil.

3

It was the first day of winter, and it was drizzling. If it had rained properly, with that dense, heavy, opaque kind of rain that blots out footprints, obscures visibility and wrecks the fragile public services, our telephone would not have rung. But it was drizzling and, at exactly six o'clock in the morning, the electricity and telephone lines in our district were operating perfectly.

Our telephone bell, which was set at full volume, made us jump out of bed. There was a frantic race along the passage from our bedrooms to the living-room. In my father's absence, it was a question of who reached the telephone first and, if she wasn't busy, my mother also joined in the stampede.

Amina caught up the receiver with one hand, and

used the other, as well as her feet, to push away the rest of the family who were jostling her. The only ones who were missing were my brother, at the other end of the line, and, of course, the new baby...

After a succession of 'What?', 'No?', 'It's not true!', 'I must be dreaming!', my sister yelped:

'Yes! Omar's got a son! Omar is a dad! We're aunties!'

My mother hurled herself on her daughter and snatched the telephone.

'Hello! Hello!' (She was shouting as though my brother was at the other end of the world.) 'Yes, my son... Is it a boy? Are you sure? Have you had a good look? A thousand Mabrouks! Well done, you apple of my eye!... Did you say four kilos?!... So what was your wife eating?... No, that's not what I meant to say?... Did you let them weigh your baby? *I don't believe it*... It doesn't matter?... You're the one who's saying that it doesn't matter, and I'm telling you that that will bring bad luck and the evil eye to the baby... Well, I'm not worried, but don't tell anyone else how heavy your son is... Did you call him Mahmoud?... Yes, I know it was your grandfather's first names, but all the same, nowadays there are such pretty name... If you'll let me, I'll call him Moud... Yes, yes... He's at sea... Oh, of course, as soon as he comes back... And Khadija?... Good... That's fine... I'll bring some soup... Above all, she must bandage her tummy properly... Your mother-in-law told her already? Good...'

When she hung up, my mother spun around and clapped her hands. Noria and Fouzia did the same. My mother and my little sisters were like little children at a funfair, and the house was filled with a festive spirit.

'I'm going to make some fritters, that will bring the baby luck,' said my mother.

Then:

'My only son has made me a grandmother. And not just any grandmother! Thank you, thank you a thousand times, O Thou the Almighty,' she intoned. 'The grandmother of a little boy who'll be a man that I shall marry off to the most beautiful girl in the world...'

Our mother, the youngest of grandmothers, was really rejoicing...

'Go, my daughters, and have your breakfast quickly and go off to school,' she said, pacing the room.

Her loose hair floated over her round shoulders, like so many waves. She flitted about, with a spring in her step, in her white housecoat. Suddenly, she stopped. Two fingers at right angles on her temple, one hand on her hip, she muttered, with her mind somewhere else:

'What am I thinking of? The soup! I'm going to make soup...'

With that she went off into the kitchen, then set about rolling up the carpet in the living-room. That morning, it was not the most urgent item on the agenda.

'Come on, come on, we must hurry,' she repeated, absent-minded once more.

She pranced to and fro. The twins came in from the kitchen with a tray, and went back, reappearing with the cups or the jam. Having dressed to go out, Noria cleaned her shoes and those of Fouzia while tirelessly singing a refrain celebrating the family bonds with the newborn baby: 'My bro-ther is a daddy and I'm an auntie, I'm an auntie, hee, hee, hee!' She left the shoes where they were, went off to her room, changed her clothes, came back and, still humming, our poetic sister went back to her chores.

My father had discovered Noria's passion for shoes when she was seven years old. Since then the task of cleaning the shoes of the whole family had fallen to her. This she did scrupulously and sometimes happily, provided she was allowed to hum...

Fouzia was still dawdling around in her nightdress. When she stopped following my mother's every move, she made a pretence of contributing to the morning chores, without saying a word. That was because on the day she was born one of my father's trawlers had caught fire and sunk (mysteriously, according to its owner), at the time of the momentous or not so momentous event, and in order to prevent her negative congenital wavelengths from travelling, my sister had been ordered to be quiet, and we had instructions to keep an eye on her. To show how happy she was, that morning she was rubbing her hands together all the while winking at Noria. It meant that she too was an aunt to the newborn baby.

A smell of burning spread through the house; the

twins had forgotten the bread which was defrosting in the oven. My mother scolded the culprits, but less severely than usual, and left the carpet half rolled-up. Standing there, in the middle of the room, she rolled her eyes as if she were looking through the walls, the chairs, the sofa, the sideboard, the table, through everything that had been the furniture of her life, looking for the thread which led her on day after day in her household duties ... The longer the inspection of the room lasted, the more the light of ecstasy was swept away from her face by her worries.

Zanouba started gurgling. I went off to fill a bottle for her and decided to stay at home to help my mother. I told her so.

'It's out of the question!' she answered as she opened the curtains.

It was the time of day when the sun diffuses the redness in the sky.

'I can skip a class ...'

'You've already messed up your nursing training and you're not going to fail some miserable typing course,' she said.

Then, harping on:

'At this rate, you'll never work and life is hard these days. Your father isn't always going to feed you ...'

There it was! Words just words, not a jot of emotion when scolding me for my failures. For if my glorious career as a nurse had not taken off, my mother did not care. My mother had never looked after us as a mother looks after her daughters; she had never worried when

21

we showed signs that we were reaching puberty, she had never explained to us what we had to protect, who or what to be afraid of, who or what we should trust...Our mother had nothing to do with the women who sat as chaperones on the banks of the Great Blue. In fact she did not look after anything: her role was restricted to repeating, copying, mimicking our father. Everything that Father stated, ordered, laid down, decided and decreed went straight in my mother's ears and imbedded itself in her neurones without being changed in the slightest. Her master's voice. That's how the twins and I described her, unknown to Noria and Fouzia, who were still too young for secrets.

As she had got married when she reached puberty, without having known her own mother, and having no sisters, no girl friends – my father would never have allowed that – it was not surprising that she knew nothing about those little chats that bond a mother and daughter. We had disembarked into the lives of my parents like a piece of bad luck. There we were and we should not have been there at all. Or at least only with the much-coveted manly protuberance, which would have made out of our procreator a father in the true sense, in other words, an honourable man. Whether consciously or not, my mother had cordoned off our relationships. To the extent that she expunged her role as a chaperone. Daughters... And we did not demand anything beyond what we were granted, an unemotional word or sentence...Never mind affection, we managed without it.

Things were different for my brother.

If my father was sorry that his son had no ambition, and scolded him violently, it was natural for my mother – affected most of all – to become really close to the apple of her eye. She treated my brother as she treated our father, often with more respect. Not only did she take care that his clothes were washed and well ironed, his socks darned and his shoes polished – even after my brother was married and he was still living with us – but she worried about his appetite and his health; the best pieces of meat were for him, and my mother would feel his forehead more than ten times an evening. With her heart in turmoil, she would wait for him to come home, and would listen for the sounds behind the bathroom door when he was in there. She was prey to foolish worries, dreading a stroke of bad luck, an accident that would take him away from her, and she did not stint in her efforts to make his happiness complete. His voice had barely broken when, at nineteen, my brother announced the news of his marriage; my father objected, my mother started a hunger strike, refused to speak and shut herself in Noria and Fouzia's room. The first time...

When he had stopped shouting, smashing the china, breaking the furniture, drinking litres of wine, threatening my mother with repudiation, to our great amazement, our father gave in. For a while, chortling in our rooms behind closed doors, we envied our brother's lot without admitting it and reversed the roles, calling our father 'his master's voice'.

My mother extracted from my father not only his blessing, but a wedding present, which was rather out of keeping with her husband's stinginess: a brand new sardine boat, four metres long, which would assure their son's future...

Having become besotted with religion, my brother had fallen under the spell of Khadija, one of my old friends, who was an expert on Qur'anic quotations. He married her the year of his baccalaureate (which he never sat, to my father's great chagrin).

As soon as she was married, Khadija in her turn gave up her typing course in order to embark on a career as a housewife and mother of a family, and when my sister-in-law left the house, which she never did without her husband, she was always veiled. As a result of witnessing the newly-wed's religious devotion, the twins and I, who, like our father, did our pious brother the disservice of showing no sign of godliness, managed to feel sufficiently guilty that we considered saying prayers. At least...

I was giving Zanouba her bottle when my mother, whose face had suddenly turned deathly pale, clutched her bosom and exclaimed:

'O God, I must go to the clinic. Now!'

I jumped.

'Who with?'

My mother never went out without my father or

24

my brother. Even with the latter, she had to get permission from the head of the family. Permission which was rarely granted...

'With a taxi,' she said as she ran towards the hall.

My sisters, who were getting ready to sit down at the table, were rooted to the spot in amazement. For a few moments, the silence could be heard; even the baby stopped sucking her bottle and the muffled rumbling from the street rose up, quickly turning into a roar. The shutters in the shop windows were lifted, the bakery took out the bread when it was only one-quarter done, the street-vendor sang his head off, trying to sell his aubergines and tomatoes...

My mother reappeared in a new pair of shoes, although her shoes were never down-at-heel, as she hardly ever had a chance to wear them...

'Now! I must go there now!' she puffed once more, out of breath, her face haggard.

'Where to?' asked Noria.

'Where to?' Fouzia repeated, forgetting to respect the rule of silence.

'You be quiet!' Amina scolded.

'I have to sprinkle salt seven times around the baby's head.'

My mother was talking to herself; we did not exist any more.

'My stupid son has let them weigh him! Can one let one's own son be weighed like a common piece of meat? By this time the whole clinic and surrounding neighbourhood will know my grandson's weight, and if I don't do the seven rounds with the salt . . . Oh no, may God preserve him for me!'

She began to moan, something she was so good at at the time:

'What have we done to you, O God Almighty, so high up, to punish us in this way ? It'll be just my luck if my grandson is struck straight away by the evil eye . . .'

'The salt can wait until Daddy comes back,' said Yasmina.

'Oh, yes, it could wait,' added Amina, whose face was as white as her mother's.

She wasn't listening. She had put on a red dress with a long skirt and long sleeves and had gathered up her dark hair into a hairband in the same shade.

'You stay at home, make the fritters and look after the baby,' she ordered me. 'I'm going to take a taxi. Oh, but I haven't got a sou . . . Has anyone got some money?' she asked, in a slightly anxious tone.

I had never known my mother to have money; she didn't need it, as my father bought everything. She never went to the hairdresser; my father danced with joy when she put henna in her hair and when she let it fall loose on her shoulders, but the idea of the hairdresser would never have entered his head. Nor hers, either. As for Turkish baths and weddings, he had forbidden them since our great-aunt had departed this life. Having been widowed at a young age, my father's aunt had not had any children. In the place of the children she never had, she had substituted my father, who in return put all his faith in her. So after his Trustworthy Man was no more, there were no more Turkish baths, no more celebrations, not even for our nearest and dearest... In any case, said our begetter, these only bring sickness and slander. Also, he proclaimed, the wife of Aziz the fisherman, the daughter-in-law of Mahmoud Zeitoun, should have nothing to do with the public baths. She had everything she needed at home: water as well as bathrooms! And six daughters to marry off would soon make her tired of weddings.

My father had had a huge bathroom built, with a wide round bath with shallow sides, so that it was like being in a public bath. And, in order to be prepared for national water cuts, he had had a two-hundred-litre water tank with an electric motor installed in the cellar.

My mother grabbed the money that I gave her. I was very keen on embroidery and from time to time I made a cloth or a sheet for a friend, but my mother knew nothing of this and didn't care where these notes came from. She slipped them into her bosom and dived into the kitchen, where she took a handful of coarse salt, wrapping it up in a handkerchief. Then she rolled herself into her white *haik*, adjusted her lace veil and, like a free woman, vanished into town.

4

When the door slammed shut, the house suddenly seemed empty and the room huge, as if the walls had receded, my great many sisters were in a dazed state, the baby seemed sleepy and much too heavy, and the silence was coated with lead.

Then Noria started to chant:

'Mo-ther's gone out, Mo-ther's left, coarse salt for the baby, the baby with the evil eye, he shouldn't have been weighed.'

'Shut up,' said Fouzia, with a lump in her throat, chewing a slice of bread and butter that she obviously no longer wanted to eat.

'My sister is jealous of my po-ems,' answered Noria, as she left the table and ran into her room.

She was swiftly followed by Fouzia who let fly at

the top of her lungs, shouting:

'It'll be my fault if the evil eye falls on Omar's son! It'll be my fault too if Mother's been disobedient. My fault! It's always my fault! Do you understand?'

I put the baby back in her cradle and joined the twins, who were clearing the breakfast table.

'Do you think Mother's gone mad?' Yasmina asked me.

'No,' I said distractedly, 'she's become a grand-mother.'

'All the same, Father's going to be drunk with rage,' said Amina.

'Father will treat her with the respect due to a grandmother. At least that's what she thinks, and I hope she isn't wrong.'

Amina gazed open-eyed.

'Do you mean that he's going to treat her like an old woman?'

'She means that he'll give her a bit of freedom,' Yasmina answered, exasperated.

Being about four or five minutes older than her twin sister, Yasmina considered herself to be the brighter of the two.

'Still, one of us should have gone with her,' said Amina, biting her lower lip. 'Alone in town . . .'

'She watches TV often enough to know how to take a taxi,' Yasmina retorted.

Then she started throwing the balcony doors and windows wide open. It had stopped drizzling and the sun ruled the sky.

29

'What do you think you're doing?' Amina asked.

'It's a dream I've had...'

'What if Father comes back,' I said.

'He'll be most welcome! Let him see that the windows are made to be opened, to be wide open!' Yasmina burst out as she inhaled the fresh air.

'If Father comes back,' said Amina, as if to make excuses for her double, 'there's no danger, because he forbade us to use the balcony because of Mother... And she's not here...'

'I think we have all lost our heads,' I said.

'And that's not all,' said Yasmina as she switched on the radio, turning the volume right up.

Another breach of Father's orders.

Mr Weather Forecast told us we would have a week of sunshine and high temperatures, and ended by hoping for rain for the sake of the farmers. Then music came on and Yasmina did a dance, clicking her fingers.

'Mo-ther's g-gone out, Mo-ther's left. Coarse s-salt for the baby. The baby with the evil eye. He shouldn't have been weighed,' Noria intoned again, her shoulders hunched under the weight of her schoolbag.

Fouzia, thinking she had already said enough, tried to keep silent, clamping her lips shut. It did not last; with the decibels carrying her along, she tapped her feet on the ground, first of all gently then louder and louder:

'*Ya chabah! Ya chabah!* Hoohooo! Long live mu-usic! Long live free-eedom!' she shouted at the top of her voice.

'Shut it,' said Amina.

She shouted so as to drown the increasing cacophony:

'What would Father do if he came back before Mother?'

'I don't know!' I shouted back.

Then I murmured:

'I'm afraid he will be back before her.'

My father would set sail before dawn and usually came home at the time when the baby had her second bottle.

Noria and Fouzia went out; the twins were not ready yet and they were going to be late. I told them so, already enjoying staying at home as mistress of the house. Yasmina turned off the radio, closed the windows and sat down.

'We're staying at home,' she said.

'It is out of the question,' I said, borrowing my mother's voice. 'You're very behind in your studies and it's not worth making things worse for yourselves,' I added hurriedly.

'Our position is already dreadful.'

'Since Mother's not here today, we can face telling someone,' Amina added, sitting down too, and folding her hands in her lap.

Then she fixed her scared doe eyes on me and continued:

'Beloved sister, would you like to listen to us, just listen?'

I steeled myself, tensing my whole body. And thus,

bravely, I prepared myself for the worst.

'So?' I asked, looking at both of them.

'We've left school,' said Yasmina, looking down at her feet.

My body relaxed; I nearly fell over backwards.

'You're no longer going to school?'

'We couldn't take it in any more,' said Yasmina again.

'Except for drawing, but that doesn't count, just drawing,' said Amina.

'Since when?'

'Since we were very small, as you know very well,' was Amina's answer.

'When did you stop the lessons?'

'More than a month ago,' Yasmina mumbled.

'That's not possible, it would have been found out, they would have written...'

'We managed to intercept the letters,' said Amina.

'Of course,' I said, with a slight shiver. 'But when you go out in the mornings,' I went on, struggling against shapeless visions, 'where do you go? What do you do with your days?'

'We go to the public gardens, sometimes to the market or a tea-room, at the far end of town. Quite often we're the only girls,' said Yasmina.

'We really can't wander the streets any more,' said Amina. 'With what's going on at the moment, we will end up being spotted. Can we rely on you to tell?'

'Tell who?'

'Mother...'

'I can't, it would be held against me, in any

case . . . You know very well what she's like . . .'

'I think she's not the same any more,' said Yasmina. 'She wouldn't have gone out alone if she hadn't changed.'

'Even if that's true, there's always Father, and he definitely hasn't changed,' I reminded them.

'If anything happened to us, not only would he hold us responsible, but he wouldn't clear up the mess like the last time,' Amina added.

'What last time are you talking about?' I said.

'You're right about Father, he'll never change,' Yasmina cut in, giving her sister a dirty look.

Then I could see my parents sitting opposite each other, our father reciting a list of all his expenditure since we were born, the money that he would have saved if we hadn't been there, worshipping the age of science and bright minds, describing my inability to tell the truth, my screwed-up nursing training, my typing course, how he had wanted me to be a do-octor, how he could never retire; the twins and how backward they were at school, that they'd end up as dressmakers – at the very best! Noria with so many faults, a sleepwalker who sooner or later would lose the power of speech. Fouzia, the bringer of bad luck, whose words sufficed to cause twenty-five per cent of the world's evils. They were all taking after me, under my bad influence . . . I could nearly hear my father's voice: They're my daughters but they've inherited stüpidity from their uncle (presumably the maternal one), Mother approving, noting . . . I could hear our

whisperings, our silences, our muffled footsteps...
These were the bad times, to make one tired of life.

'Mother would go on a hunger strike,' said Amina
suddenly.

I stared at my sister and wondered whether my
father wasn't right.

'A hunger strike for you?'

'She's done one for you,' he said again.

There was a heavy weight in the pit of my stomach.

'She won't do that,' I said. 'Not for you or for me, if
it comes to that...'

Then, almost angrily:

'For her to go on one, we'd have to be called Omar
or Mahmoud.'

'But what will become of us?' asked Amina, raising
her arms.

'Just think of what you'd like... Go to a training
school...'

'For dressmaking,' said Yasmina. 'We'll go to a
dressmaking school.'

'Even Father said that we'll be dressmakers,' said
Amina. 'So we'll do some sewing...'

'Sewing?'

'You're good at embroidery,' Amina murmured.

My voice was shaking with anxiety, of the type that
arouses sisterly love.

'But would you like to do sewing? Would you
know how to do it?' They raised their eyebrows and
widened their eyes as if my question held all the
complications in the world. It was after nine o'clock,

my mother had gone out (alone), she who only knew the clinics and hospitals by name, she who had her babies at home, like a Red Indian woman, sometimes with the clumsy help of her elders. My mother, who bandaged herself after her miscarriages in the wash-house, her body draining itself relentlessly and without the slightest regret for the blood of her womb, that blood which caused angels to get angry, she used to say resignedly; my sisters who were wandering the streets...and the clamour which was rising, swelling, which would soon flow to our door, bringing us news of earthquakes and volcanoes stirring.

Yasmina started to cry.

'I don't even know which finger to put a thimble on.'

I took her by the hand.

'I know. But you can learn. You can learn anything. And maybe you'd even like sewing...'

'Drawing, we do like drawing,' said Amina, crying too.

'But no one will take us seriously,' said Yasmina.

'In any case, there's no school for that,' was Amina's comment.

'There's the Fine Arts School,' I said.

'We wrote to them,' was Amina's retort.

'But they only take graduates,' said Yasmina.

They started to weep. At the same rate, with the same sniffing and the same sound. The shortest day of the year was starting to be interminable...

Downstairs, the garage door slammed shut. Yasmina

held back her tears, turned her head and blurted out:

'Father!'

Like an echo, Amina cried out: 'Fa–ather!'

Faster than lightning, the twins went up the stairs leading to my brother's flat, where they took refuge.

5

His hippopotamus shape was silhouetted on the staircase, standing out clearly against the light of the hall, then vanished into the kitchen. Zanouba cried for another bottle.

'Nayla! Nayla!' he shouted.

Then:

'I've brought some red mullet, just the kind you like – small and very pink. Come quickly, they're still moving.'

When I went into the kitchen with the baby in my arms, my father was helping himself to wine. As soon as he saw me, an unusual sight at this time of day, his narrow eyes grew wide, then shrank. He drank his wine without taking his eyes off us. A moment later, with his glass in one hand, wiping his lips with the back of the other, he said:

'Where is your mother?'

'Well...' I stammered.

' Well, what?' he asked, keeping a burp down with difficulty.

His left eye was twitching and he was grinding his teeth quietly: he was being overtaken by anxiety.

My father had a sort of sixth sense, undoubtedly rooted in superstitions that were firmly held and consciously maintained. He was not really keen on religion, I don't remember ever having seen him pray or even go to the mosque on a holy day, and, if he fasted during Ramadan, this was more to save money and due to habit than for Allah or his familiars; if my mother, under my brother's influence, tried to restore his faith, my father would snub her and discourage her by his little mocking giggles, reminding her about the achievements of mankind, as well as his own: open-heart and laser surgery, Concorde between Paris and New York, walking on the moon, underwater tunnels, faxes and satellites, missiles and surgical warfare... But just as his aunt and his sailor's life had taught him, my father lived by watching signs: he watched shooting stars, and at each new moon shook his banknotes in the moonlight so that that his fortune would increase; he never went to sea on the thirteenth day of the month; he never lit a cigarette by the light of a candle, as that would cause a sailor's life to be lost; he clapped when glass was broken; he would chase the black cats who came into our garden, with a broomstick, he would shut himself into the house if he happened to hear an owl hooting or if the sole of his left foot was itchy; he burned incense to celebrate the purchase of a boat, or the day after a nightmare – nightmares that he described loudly in the bathroom as he used the toilet and pulled the chain a few times; he valued his children according to the luck, or bad luck, that they could bring him . . . If he had not been so well known in this part of town, a town of fishermen and big shipowners, our father would happily have consulted fortune-tellers and other psychics.

'Where is she?'

My reply mattered little to him. In fact, I didn't make one. It was stuck in my throat or a bit lower down. He threw down his glass, which smashed on the ground, then ran out of the kitchen, rushing around like a madman, calling my mother at the top of his voice. He tripped on the half-rolled-up carpet, pulled himself together and went on looking for her, swearing by all the saints to smash the house to atoms and to turn my mother and all the women in the world into dust. When he had gone into all the rooms in the house, bathrooms and wash-house included, when he had smashed everything that fell under his hands – even the precious imported Lexdura glasses, which were supposed to be unbreakable, could not survive – when he had torn my mother's dresses, as well as our own if they were there, he stopped howling and running about. With weary steps, he came back to the kitchen, where I was still sitting, my feet rooted to the ground, the baby held firmly against my chest.

With sweat pouring down his face, breathing unevenly, he sat down. He grabbed the bottle of wine, dropped the cork and drank straight from the bottle. Then he lit a cigarette and dragged on it without exhaling. In a voice that pretended to be calm, he asked:

'Where is she?'

He let the smoke emerge from his nose and stared at me.

My tongue went dry, swelled up, grew heavy and tied itself in knots as my father's eyes filled with blood, like the eyes of a torturer about to get to work . . . My jaws were clamped together, my teeth were grinding, grinding to the point of cracking . . . Then the fear of stirring up his wrath, which he would have to pour out on me and the baby, reactivated my saliva glands. At last my tongue unwound itself, but my mind was still in turmoil.

'Omar's wife has had a baby – and it's a boy. Omar has called him pappy, oh, no, grandfather, I mean Mahmoud,' I reeled off.

The breathing of myself, Zanouba and my father, the dripping tap, the humming fridge – the slightest noise hit my eardrums, and echoed like a dreadful racket.

'Good, but that doesn't tell me where Nayla is,' he said in that voice which demanded peace in the world and in our homes.

Then he threw his cigarette in the sink and jumped out of his chair. With his hands flat on the table, his body at right angles and his face almost brushing my own, he roared:

'Where's your mother, for God's sake?'

Incessantly invoking God's name, with the back of his hand he swept both the crate of red mullet and the bottle off the table. The new baby, who had not yet become used to the explosions of her father's voice, to fish flying about the house, or floods of wine, bawled her little lungs out. I held her tightly against my chest and started to rock myself as though to the beat of wild music.

'At the clinic, because of the salt, he weighs four kilos and nobody knows what his mother was eating, the evil eye...'

My exhausted little sister dozed off and in the end I made myself understood. My father rushed towards the door, the noise of footsteps was deadened on the stairs, my legs trembled, the ground opened up, siroccos wrapped themselves around me and lifted me up... Was the beginning of the end of the world so disturbing?

Had he gone to look for my mother? What was he going to do? Beat her to pulp, and us as well? Would her new status of grandmother save us? Maybe he was just going to a bar to quench his rage and celebrate his first grandson's birth...

The baby moved in my arms and moaned slightly to remind me she was hungry. I shook off my torpor.

Now the house was a battlefield and I called the twins to my aid. They refused to come out of their hiding-place, being convinced that their father would be back at any moment.

Zanouba was drinking her milk ravenously when my mother and Omar came back. My mother was out of breath and dripping with perspiration. She uncovered her face and wiped her brow and neck with the lace veil.

'He's as beautiful as a spring day,' she said, towering with pride, her pupils dilated with excitement.

She did not seem to be worried about the broken glass, the torn clothes, upside-down furniture, or indeed to notice the havoc in our house.

Omar spoke up:

'What happened here?'

'Father was in a temper. He's just gone out,' I mumbled, without looking up. My mother let her veil fall, stepped over a few chairs and flopped onto the sofa. There was a smell of fish and spilt wine coming from the kitchen.

'Oh, my God!' she exclaimed, with a raised eyebrow.

Then she remembered the existence of our governor.

'Why did he do that?' asked Omar.

'He was looking for Mother.'

My brother's face clouded over.

'Why was he looking for you?'

With her hand on her breast, my mother drew her breath in, then breathed out, murmuring slightly. She took a long look around the room; she was obviously counting the cost of the damage and of her husband's rage.

The rings under her eyes gradually turned purple.

'Why was he looking for you?' my brother repeated.

'I thought I'd be home before him,' my mother murmured.

'Then it wasn't he who dropped you off...'

'It couldn't wait... You know, the salt... Anyway, why should he reproach me? He would have done the same thing himself, if not more so...'

'But who went with you in the taxi?' asked Omar.

'Our neighbour, you know, Youssef Allouchi. He saw me on the pavement trying to hail a taxi, then he stopped one for me, and kindly offered to come with me. Also, I must think about paying him back, since he paid for the trip...'

'My God,' said my brother. 'She went out alone. Without his leave...'

'So? That was going to happen one day!' my mother suddenly protested.

Then a bit more quietly:

'After all, I wasn't going to stay young for ever.'

The colour came back into her cheeks, and her features relaxed: so where did our young begetter get this sudden self-confidence from? Was she expecting Omar to support her now that he was a father, with powers strengthened by the arrival of this new protuberance? In any case, I applauded silently; my mother was at last standing up to the thing that had controlled her whole life – pregnancies alternating with housework.

Unable to stay in hiding any longer, the twins risked making an appearance. Nobody took any notice of them and when they began to explain why they were there – they claimed that they were there to clear up the mess – nobody listened to them. They looked quickly at each other, breathed a sigh of relief and slipped into the kitchen, almost on tiptoe.

'All the same, he didn't need to turn the house into a pigsty,' said my brother, looking around the room.

Just then, the front door banged on its hinges, the walls shook. Then the house was wrapped in a funereal silence on a moonless night. My father appeared. Hatred, or something stronger than hatred which was unknown to me, poured from his brow, his nose and his chin, and contorted his features. As he stood there, one arm hanging beside his body, an index finger pointing towards my mother, his eyes glued to the ground, he took a deep breath, then, without any preamble and quite calmly, he repudiated her. Three times. It was like the end of the world.

With her elbows resting on her knees, her head between her hands, my mother did not flinch. She looked down at her feet gravely, her eyelids heavy, and gradually a grin screwed up her face into a wicked smile. Omar banged his temples with both his fists, then in turn he became rooted to the spot. For a long time he stared at my father's quivering pot-belly.

'There is only one God,' he mumbled incessantly.

The twins were standing in the kitchen doorway, their mouths wide open, looking bewildered, as if they were afraid to understand.

Suddenly, my brother demanded:

'Why three times?'

'Yes. Why three times?' my father repeated, his cheeks deathly pale, his eyes filled with disgust, his nose large and red.

He leaned against the wall. Then, just as our dead great-aunt would have done, he let himself slip and collapsed, his legs straight out, his feet touching, his hands flat on the tiles. As he looked for a rescuing sign – which was not to be found on the face of his ex-wife or that of his male heir – he grabbed the little hair he had left and started to pull it out.

'I am dogged by misfortune,' he groaned.

Zanouba burped.

'Well,' my mother said coldly. 'I'm going to bundle up my things and move in with my son.'

My father jumped up.

'You're not budging from here!' he shouted at her.

'What does that mean?' said my brother.

'We can be remarried. Immediately!'

'That's out of the question,' answered Omar, shaking his head.

'You've repudiated her three times and you weren't even angry.'

'And you are not the Imam Al-Ghazali!' my father

scolded him. 'Our Imam will tell me what to do.'

'He'll tell you that it's only possible if she contracts a second marriage, then obviously there must be a second repudiation. That's the law.'

'Well, then, we'll apply to the law,' said my father. And he left.

part two

part two

6

My father complained that his lunch was indigestible –
a sardine stew cooked by the twins – and he threatened
to make them swallow a bottle of bleach if his ulcer
came to life again. With his hand on his stomach, and
with slobbering lips, he went to take up his post on the
stairs, his ears cocked. From time to time, he glanced
over his shoulder, to make sure that he would not be
caught listening to the noises from the floor above,
where his ex-wife was waiting for her son.

In the house across the road, in the presence of my
mother's fiancé, the Imam and the two witnesses,
Omar, the accepted legal guardian, was blessing the
wedding. Like the morning after a nightmare, my
father was showing all the signs of being overwhelmed
by worry. However, had he not organized this

wedding himself? Had he not dug up and handsomely rewarded the two witnesses, engaged the services of the young widow, who lived at the corner of our street, to act as my mother's chaperone?

Without knowing exactly what he was afraid of, nor being able to spot anything which could throw light upon it, in the end he ended his vigil and returned to his digestive problems. Then he started pacing the house, avoiding the bedroom which was no longer conjugal and which still smelled of patchouli, despite the three months which had passed since my mother was repudiated.

That day, my sisters and I were forbidden to stay at Omar's. But when his pain had been subdued, my father stopped whinging and told me to come up – if I felt like it. In fact, this was really an order, one not open to discussion, which you cannot get out of or escape from. He asked me, somehow or other, to spy on my mother as she prepared for her second nuptials. Maybe she was pleased about it, after all ... What portent was bringing him so much worry?

When I came into the bedroom, my sister-in-law was trying to persuade my mother to swap her dress for a caftan from Khadija's wedding trousseau. My mother, as exhausted as if she had been staying in a concentration camp, let herself be persuaded into the rustle of the gold-trimmed caftan. Afterwards, nobody will ever know why, Khadija offered to do her make-up. Without a word, my mother shot her a look emanating from the depths of hell.

My imperturbable sister-in-law suggested that she could at least outline her eyes with kohl.

'Allah is beautiful and loves beauty,' she said, as though she were the mother of all believers.

Zanouba and Mahmoud, lying close together in the same cot, answered in cheerful baby-talk.

'All the same, it's not a funeral,' my sister-in-law added casually.

She opened the bottle of kohl and started stirring the powder with the little sharp stick.

'Why are you laughing at me?' my mother burst out then.

She spun round and faced my sister-in-law.

'Have I ever mistreated you or humiliated you?' she shouted, sniffing back her tears and pushing her daughter-in-law away.

Khadija dropped the bottle and the khol spilt on my mother's clothes and the carpet.

'What have I done? Oh, what have I done?' wailed the daughter-in-law. 'Why is there so much bad feeling? Is it not Thy will, O Thou who pours solace on all the afflicted?' she continued as she tidied up the wedding clothes and cosmetics.

Then she locked herself in the bathroom, where she bemoaned her ruined caftan and the harshness of mothers-in-law.

'Drawn by the shouts of one and the wails of the other, making the most of a moment when my father's attention had strayed, Noria and Fouzia slipped into the bedroom. My mother wiped her eyes, blew her nose loudly and stopped crying. But she wore that same solemn expression that had stamped her features the day she was repudiated. My little sisters, motionless and silent like people who feel guilty, were watching her. Then, suddenly full of energy, she moved a chair, straightened a cushion and scraped off the specks of kohl on the wedding dress... And her eyes were sparkling in a strange way, her mind seemed to be light-years from here. She had almost ceased to be Nayla Zeitoun.

My mother was still pretty at the age of thirty-seven. Not the births, or the hard labour, or the harrowing pain, or her life as a recluse had in any way affected her soft skin, her milky complexion, her good head of hair, her flashing eyes set with thick, curly lashes, her statuesque figure and her flat tummy... A beauty which her children – except perhaps my brother – had not managed to inherit, our originator's genes having prevailed unchallenged.

Our brother's voice reached us from the front door. In less than a second, my mother wrapped herself in her daughter-in-law's ivory silk veil, put on her red shoes and clattered down the stairs. Without a look at us. Without a goodbye. Even forgetting her baby.

When they awoke from their hypnosis, Noria and Fouzia ran after her. The former, a victim's whine in her voice, asked if she could accompany Mother, and the latter asked the same thing, in her own way, using gestures that were no less martyr-like. But my mother, her white, graceful silhouette cutting the night in two, was already a long way off.

7

I went over to the cot when Khadija came out of her hiding-place, with the scowl on her face that she wore every time we found ourselves alone together.

'Leave the baby here,' she commanded. 'I'll look after her until your mother comes back.'

Since she had no wish for complicity I avoided being in league in any way with my brother's wife.

'My mother has got married again,' I said.

'Your mother is coming back in a week's time, at the latest. Everyone knows about your father's shenanigans ... Even my poor husband has got involved in it. Much against his will,' she sighed.

I left her, my ears ringing with her honeyed voice singing praises to God, pleading for his mercy and pity for Zeitoun, the father, and his daughters.

The house lay plunged in semi-darkness, as though the electric current had been reduced and the curtains had lost their sheen. Like little grey mice, we slipped between the pieces of furniture, rubbed against the walls, with our lips tightly sealed. The twins vanished into the kitchen, where they heated up what was left of the lunchtime stew and improvised a dish to settle our father's stomach. In one corner of the room, Noria and Fouzia pretended to do their homework, with their necks sunk between their thin little shoulders. My father turned off the television and opened the balcony doors wide. A gentle spring breeze tried in vain to blow away the brown tobacco smoke from the cigarettes that he chain-smoked. Across the road, our neighbour's house sparkled with all the lights on and the smell of lamb couscous, mingled with the scent of jasmin, wafted on the air.

My father gazed at the sky, watching for a shooting star, then he murmured chants in which only the names of my mother and my great-aunt could be heard. Just then a moth landed on his shoulder. His face lit up and his whole body stiffened.

'Hey, you two,' he whistled. 'Come over here. Quietly.'

Noria and Fouzia obeyed him, guessing what he was going to ask them.

'Catch him,' he whispered. 'Just catch this moth . . . ge-e-ently.'

The moth fluttered its wings furiously, leaving in its wake my sisters who were petrified with confusion as they waited to be scolded by their father. Postponing the scene he was going to make, he started chasing the insect, which went to settle inside a lamp. Discouraged but in a calm mood, he turned on the television again, avoiding the news – when and why had our father decreed that the world would turn upside-down without us? – and let himself be soothed by the drone of the synchronized voices of an American film on TV.

He did not get off the sofa, nor did he touch his milk couscous. The twins stuffed themselves under the horrified gaze of the youngest members of the family, who were not only sickened by the sardine stew, but flabbergasted by the appetite of their elders on the day that our mother was settling into a new home.

As soon as we reached our bedrooms, we could hear music and ululations. Moving as one, my father, Yasmina and I flung ourselves on to the terrace and leaned over the railing. Neighbours and staff from the Town Hall were gathering in the garden opposite us.

The celebrations were in full swing at Youssef Allouchi's house.

'The traitor,' my father grumbled.

'That means nothing at all,' I said, dodging my sister's efforts to kick me.

She was warning me to be quiet, for what was the point of speaking to a man on the edge of a nervous breakdown, who moreover never confided in his daughters.

However, in a rather thin voice, King Solomon mumbled:

'Do you think so?'

Above us, the moon grew round, turned pink, like a pregnant woman, and smiled with the blessing of the angels.

'They're celebrating so that there won't be any suspicion,' I said, my face very red and my heart like a leaf torn off its branch, disputed by winds from the four corners of the earth.

'Well, well,' said my father, thus putting an end to this . . . attempt at complicity.

He closed the balcony door on the sobs of a lute drowning the familiar and no less langorous lament of the nightingale of the newly-wed.

My father lay down on the sofa, as still as a corpse.

My mother was being married again.

Just like the times during my mother's confinements, we gathered in the twins' room, which was the largest and furthest away. Moving like oppressed people, we unrolled the mattresses and took blankets and pillows out of the cupboards. In a soft light, reassured by the calm reigning in the house, we whispered as if we were at the theatre.

'Why did Mother cry so much?' asked Noria.

'Because she's afraid on account of not being a virgin and that might cause a bit of a scandal,' Amina sniggered.

'That's not funny,' said Yasmina.

'What's a v-virgin?' Noria asked, obviously interested in the twin's lesson.

'Just like you are,' said Amina again, teasing. 'At least, that's what we hope you are,' she added.

She chuckled under her breath.

'I would love to have been with her,' said Fouzia.

'To eat lamb or to take advantage of Mr Allouchi's learning?' Amina hiccupped.

'Calm down,' said Yasmina. 'Father's going to hear you giggling.'

'Fouggia is so si-ick of fish, especially sardines, and so-o am I.'

Then:

'But the marriage is a sham and there can't be lamb.'

'I smelt the meat,' Fouzia protested. 'But I've never been to a wedding.'

'Not allowed,' said Amina. 'We're not even allowed to go to our own mother's wedding.'

'Sham. A sham wed-ding,' Noria persisted.

'Why don't you sing something instead of saying silly things?' Yasmina asked her as she ran her hand through her hair.

'I don't have the heart, si-ster, not the heart.'

'Let's get on, we must get on as Mother's going to be back really soon,' I said. 'While we're waiting, hum a little tune for us, that's your trick.'

'I don't have the heart, si-ster, not the heart.'

'Please do, she's coming back,' Amina joined in.

Then, as she burst out laughing:

'She's just gone to keep an appointment, over there in our neighbour's house, just a change of scene. That's what people of her age often do, they want a change of air, they like to have a good time. Even though it's Father who gave his blessing.'

Then with a solemn expression and a serious voice she went on:

'As he never wants her to go to parties, he's managed to organize one specially in her honour... Just like Aziz Zeitoun...'

'We're the laughing stock of the district,' Yasmina chipped in.

'This morning the baker asked me to congratulate Father and my charming family, including yourself, and wished me as good a match as Mother's. His customers burst out laughing!' Amina blurted out.

'People have said thi-ings like that to me-e and I know that's why Mother's crying.'

'I don't give a damn about those people,' I muttered.

'But everybody knows that Allouchi's going to divorce Mother and Father's going to marry her again,' Yasmina announced.

'And if Allouchi doesn't repudiate her? If he really married her?' Fouzia let slip.

'You only open your mouth to spit out bile,' Amina scolded her.

'That can't happen. He's married already,' Yasmina interrupted.

'To who?' asked Noria, holding back her tears, her eyes betraying joy.

'To the jinnee – that's well known,' Yasmina answered.

'Wha-at's a jinnee?'

'A Chinese lady,' Amina chipped in again.

'It's a woman from a world inhabited by God's creatures who see us, but we can't see them. And just like all human beings, they are capable of the worst horrors and of the noblest deeds,' Yasmina explained.

Then, smiling broadly:

'But whether they're in the camp of the good or the bad genies, the jinnees don't approve of joint wives or concubines. Even if they are of the same mould.'

'Do you mean that Mother belongs to the jinnees?' Fouzia exclaimed.

'It doesn't mean anything of the kind. And all you've got to do, is listen. Words aren't for your ears! For twelve years you've been told that, for God's sake!' Amina retorted.

'She means that Mother's going to come back,' I said.

8

Lurching and belching from the wine, my father wandered about the house; his footsteps now echoed in the passageway. We kept very quiet, listening for the slightest noise, as we waited for the house to be destroyed immediately. That's when he opened the bedroom door. We sat up, gripped by fear. The time must have come for him to accuse us of all evils, to thrash us, to the point of death and fainting.

But our father's plump face was cracked by a smile. A penitent smile, admittedly, but a smile. Even his red, puffy, half-closed eyes seemed to be swimming in sad mirth. So what had become of the roars of the drunken lion? What fear had come into the head of the man who could buy and sell the district together with its inhabitants?

Unsteadily, he sat down on the edge of a bed. For a moment, he peered at us with one eye. Then, after clearing his throat a few times, he launched into an endless oath, which he finished off by giving each of us a kind word. He swore on the graves of his father, his mother, his aunt, his grandfathers and grandmothers, male and female saints, in front of us, his daughters, his best witnesses, that he would stop drinking, the very next day; that he would go and cleanse his soul and his bones at Zamzam, the water source at the holy Kaaba; that my mother would go with him; that they would bring us back dress lengths of damask and Indian silk, even jewellery for our wedding trousseaus.

Sitting there, he paused for a moment, his open eye blinked and the other half-opened, then his shiny head reflected the room's soft light. Did he know what these luxury items would cost him?

He cleared his throat again and, tugging his earlobe, he continued with his monologue, giving Fouzia permission to speak from now on, to hold forth if she pleased and, yes, even to sing – she could sing at the top of her voice if she wanted: after all, he wasn't down to his last boat or his last misfortune. He absolved Noria from her shoe-cleaning chores, promised to buy poetry and song books for her, even a piano, to engage a speech therapist for her; he described a new plan for the twins' future...

'You're going to be hairdressers. I'll buy you a salon that the best architects from the capital will transform into a salon worthy of the Parisian hairdressers.'

'Thank you, Father.'

'Thank you, Father.'

'Tha-ankk you, Father.'

'Thank you, Father.'

'As for you,' he continued looking straight at me, 'I'll get the cleverest marabout in the country to rid you of the devil inside you.'

Seeing the funny side of this, I looked at the twins, who immediately looked down, so that they could glue their eyes to some object of interest.

'I'm sure you're a good girl,' my father went on. 'After all, you'd be a good girl if it weren't for this bad genie. When you're better, when you've atoned for your faults, when you've been trained, I'll buy computers, faxes, photocopiers and everything you need for the most modern office.'

'Thank you, Father,' I said in turn.

I tried again to meet my sisters' eyes. They had not stirred and raised their eyebrows sadly.

'Agreed?' said my father, letting out a belch that smelt strongly of wine.

'Agreed!'

'Agreed!'

'Agreed!'

'Agreed!'

'Agreed...'

'All right, all right,' he said.

He got up. Before turning on his heel, he said triumphantly:

'I found the moth. I put it under a glass, so be good and don't let it escape, as it's a present for your mother. To thank her for being so brave.'

And he mumbled:

'After all, she didn't want this marriage.'

The door closed on silence and stupor. It was drizzling in the street.

'Was that Father?'

'Father's drunk. He's very drunk.'

'May God bring Mother back soon,' Yasmina pleaded as she switched off the light. 'Very soon.'

Then we all chorused:

'Amen. Amen indeed.'

But what was it that was inside me? What fault did I have to atone for? My father certainly couldn't take wine.

There were gunshots tearing the night apart. I leapt out of my bed. I put on the light and went over to the window. It was after midnight. Overhead, there was somebody walking around. My sisters were sound asleep. Noria, who took care to tie herself down in her bed, was lisping in her slumber of frustrated sleep-walking. Fouzia, whose adenoids had not yet been removed, was snoring with clenched fists. Their legs intertwined, their eyelids fluttering at exactly the same time, the twins were floating in the same land of dreams.

I pricked up my ears. No more shooting. I had had

a dream. There was no doubt of that. I went back to bed and buried my head under the blankets. As soon as sleep overtook me, a wedding party against a backdrop of shooting assailed my eyelids. A wicked genie had his hand on the trigger. Under the helpless eye of Aziz the fisherman.

9

Next day, we were awakened by the weekly prayers and the sun which was piercing our slatted shutters. My mother, who insisted on everything being done by ten o'clock, the time when my father came home from the market, would not have liked this deviation from old habits. And even if worship were not written into our marching orders, even if the neighbours had no right to watch the way we lived, even if for the last three months my mother had lived with her son, it was as if . . .

The lights in the kitchen and the living-room had been on all night. The TV was switched to Hexagon's Channel One – since the repudiation, my father had joined the audience of I-divorce-you, you-divorce-me. Or something like that.

No sign of our father around the house. Could he be still at the market?

It took Noria and Fouzia no time at all to find him in the loggia. Wearing his only pair of underpants, with his fat hairy body squeezed between a box of potatoes and a jerrycan of water, our father was sleeping the sleep of the just. Empty wine bottles rolled around at his feet. A smell of vomit rose from his bed of fortune. We awakened him with our noise. He blinked his eyes and opened them with difficulty.

'Nayla,' he mumbled.

Was he still dreaming?

Then, with a threatening look:

'Where is she? Where's your mother?'

'Is she com-ing home today?' Noria asked, eyes wide with happiness.

Would local opinion not find it blatant if she came back to her first home no sooner than she had entered her second one?

Squinting at Fouzia, he said:

'Omar, my bullshitting son, where has your mother gone?'

'To the wedding,' was Fouzia's reply. 'Don't you remember?'

My father only remembered what he wanted to; he shouted:

'I'll cut off your allowance, you son of an imbecile!'

Fouzia, who believed in life and its wonderful reversals and was filled with an unquenchable need to sing at the top of her voice, had no intention of letting her father depart from the promises and permissions given the previous night.

With a wild gesture, she went on:

'You know about the wedding. The sham wedding, because that's the will of the Chinese lady.'

At once, my father recovered his fierceness.

'Out of my sight! Bad-luck charm for bad luck! Get out of my life! Pyromaniac! Mother-killer! Aunt-killer!' he bellowed.

Sensing the danger, Noria pulled Fouzia by the arm, to tell her she must stop. But Fouzia did not take her sister's hint seriously and only kept quiet after the loud slap that laid her out on the floor.

My father stepped over his daughter and charged into the house, his soft, heavy buttocks slapping together. Right in the middle of the terrace, ignoring his half-naked state and the people watching him behind their windows, he started doing exercises, which he suddenly stopped in order to take a good look at the newly-weds' home. It seemed to be empty. Or inhabited by too many people, my father whinnied.

'Last night he went as far as firing a gun and this morning he's sleeping in,' he said.

As he was throwing himself into an abusive tirade against the underdogs and the fortunate of the whole world, Khadija interrupted him. There were blue rings around her eyes and her translucent lips were as pale as her face.

When she saw my father wriggling and quibbling,

she turned on her heel as quietly as she had come.

'How can I ask for help from a man who hasn't got a human face any more? God will come to my aid, only God will come to my aid,' she mumbled.

As her visits to our house were confined to emergencies, I thought that one of the little ones was ill. I caught her on the landing.

'What's the matter, Khadija? Is Zanouba ill? Is Moud all right?'

'Mahmoud,' she corrected me, opposed to life's informalities.

Then:

'Mahmoud and Zanouba are fine. It's Omar. He didn't come home.'

For a moment, I could not speak; this was definitely not my brother's usual behaviour.

'Where do you think he is?'

'There were shots fired during the night,' she said. 'He'll never come back. Dead or alive, they'll never give him back to me.'

In spite of her cold, stubborn manner, I tried to comfort her.

'I heard the shots. And Father did too. But it was at Allouchi's house, for the wedding,' I said. 'Omar has definitely gone fishing; he had to go straight after the party, which ended rather late,' I added.

'I know what I'm talking about,' she said.

'What are you talking about?'

She was withdrawing from me. I caught hold of her arm.

'God knows everything,' she said.

'Yes,' I said. 'But what do you know that we don't know?'

She released her arm from my grip and for the first time since she had come to our house, this woman who had been a friend of mine looked me straight in the eye.

'Why are you not sorry?' she asked abruptly.

'For what?'

'For what you did, fooling other people, including your own brother, who thinks he has to take his revenge and is doing so against his better judgment.'

She said nothing for a moment. Then, without letting me say a word, she continued:

'God is just, I'll pray for him to have mercy on my husband and the soul of your child.'

I watched her go upstairs with a step from beyond the grave. How should I answer this raving? Which of the two of us was becoming unhinged?

Whatever the reply, that was the day when madness materialized in our home.

10

My father chain-smoked, drank coffee, ate milk couscous, without taking his eyes off our neighbour's house, from which nothing leaked out. At nightfall, the street lights did not come on and the neighbour-hood was swallowed up in disturbing gloom.

When finally my father left the terrace in order to shut himself in the bathroom, we managed to speak again and I asked Yasmina to go and find out whether my brother was back. She returned a few moments later, with Zanouba in her arms.

'Mother has forgotten her,' she said.

'Oh, that's normal,' giggled Amina.

'And Omar?' I asked.

'He hasn't come home yet,' said Yasmina. 'I'll have to go back there to fetch Moud,' she added as she unloaded the baby into my arms.

'Why are you going back for Moud?'

'His mother has to go out.'

'Where?'

'Probably to go and look for her husband.'

'Khadija is on the point of losing her reason,' I said.

Then I described what she had told me on the landing. My sisters looked at me long and hard, with something close to sadness darkening their pupils.

'I'm afraid it's very serious,' I said.

I broke the silence with a short laugh.

'Pray for the soul of my child? My brother is avenging me...she's really not well...'

'Yes, yes,' said Yasmina. 'No doubt. I'm going to fetch Moud.'

'What's this about her leaving?' I asked Amina.

'How do I know? Maybe she's going to see her mother...'

'Or to the Knackers' Yard,' said Fouzia.

'You have no right to talk about that,' Amina blurted out. 'Father would have your scalp if he heard you.'

'She's mad. Khadija is out of her mind. Pray for the soul of my child, I can't get over it,' I said once more, trying in vain to make sense of my sister-in-law's words.

'Omar can't keep his mouth shut,' Fouzia whispered as she tickled Zanouba.

Noria was staring at me with her mouth wide open.

'Nor I, I ca-an't remember anything,' she yawned.

Visions of horror and imperceptible memories struck my frontal lobes. Then for a while, my sisters started to tango and vibrate as though they were shaken by an invisible force. When I wanted to intervene, not knowing which one to catch first, I collapsed, my head full of Zanouba's bawling.

11

In a distorting mirror, a girl in a white blouse, who
looks like my double, says to a man who is the spitting
image of Aziz Zeitoun, my father:

'I am not to blame for this . . . We were kidnapped
on our way out of the hospital.'

My father's retort, with raised eyebrows, pursed lips:

'And what did they do to you, these abductors?'

'They took us to the Knackers' Yard . . .'

But the man gets irritated. He interrupts:

'Apart from that, what did they do to you ? Because
I haven't had wind of a ransom demand, and in any
case I wouldn't have paid up.'

'They weren't asking for money.'

He boomed:

'What did they do to you?'

'They raped some of us and cut the throats of the others.'

'But you! What did they do to you, the so-called nurse in the service of the feeble?'

'They cut my throat,' the young girl then replies. Without batting an eyelid.

The man relaxes a bit. He claps for a long time; a shiver of pride adorns his moustache. Suddenly, he stiffens. With an unbelieving eye, and a closed look, he looks in amazement at the girl's tummy, which is becoming surprisingly large. She seems to see what is filling her through her skin. I too wanted to look inside this tummy which grew rounder and rounder, but Yasmina's voice and little kisses put a stop to my curiosity.

In the soft light of the bedroom, I could just make out my sister's face, and the dream had already faded into the limbo of memory.

'Are you all right?' she asked.

'Oh, yes.'

That was true, I did feel well, and light as air, as though I had been relieved of a burden whose nature was unknown to me.

'It took three of us to get you to bed. Even though you're as thin as a rake. I think you must have low blood pressure or something like that,' she said. 'As you fell over, you nearly hurt Zanouba; she just got a little bump on her forehead.'

'And Omar?'

'Still not home and Father is still in the bathroom.'

'Any news from the house across the road?'

'There have been a few tremors. Nothing serious, but the neighbourhood is in total darkness: a general power-cut. We didn't even hear the evening prayers. Ours is the only house with lights on, and our generator is beginning to run out. On top of that, it's raining cats and dogs.'

There was a roll of thunder.

'Let's go over to Allouchi's,' I said as I got out of bed.

'The phone is cut off.'

'Then let's go out, let's go and see what's happening over there.'

'You can't be serious...'

'Oh, yes, I am.'

'And Father? What are you going to do with Father? And you must eat, you haven't had a bite all day. You're going to pass out again.'

'I'll do what I like about Father and I'll eat later.'

Driving rain was lashing the town. Yasmina followed me grudgingly, grinding her teeth. Our windows were still open, on the orders of the head of the family. Then the storm stopped. The sky cleared. The air grew fresh. The town was moving slowly under a moon which was about to burst forth.

I moved stealthily towards the bathroom. And just as my late great-aunt and my mother would have done, I stuck my ear to the door. Our father's coughing interrupted by mumbles reassured us, but without letting us know what he was plotting.

'Witchcraft,' said Yasmina.

We exchanged knowing looks and I bent down to the keyhole. Wearing his only pair of underpants, and sitting on the bare marble, Aziz Zeitoun was looking at the moth which was wedged against the sides of the upturned glass. I felt weak and drew back, letting my sister take my place.

'It's not serious,' she mumbled, with a shrug of her shoulders. 'We've seen him do worse than that.'

'But that's not even witchcraft!'

'So what? He's going a bit round the bend. It'll pass off.'

'I'm going to have a word with him.'

'What are you going to say?'

'You'll see. If there's a bad reaction, we won't take the risk of going to Allouchi's.'

I leaned my forehead against the door and, without knowing why, I tried to imitate the tones of my great-aunt. I whispered:

'Apple of my brother's eye, speak to me. Speak to your aunt.'

Yasmina pulled me roughly by my arm and without letting any sound come out of her mouth, her lips formed the words:

'*Crackers. You're really crackers.*'

Just then, my father's voice called out:

'Whoever has cursed me has recited his grievances one by one at the crack of dawn.'

Then he groaned:

'Save me, O my dear aunt, tell me what to do.'

We took two leaps backwards and scampered off, pursued by a ghost.

Later on in the night, while Yasmina and I were having trouble getting off to sleep, my father came out of the shadows. Wrapped in a bath towel, and close-shaven, he reeked of eau-de-Cologne, as if for a big party.

'I've got to go across the road,' he said. 'One of you has to come with me.'

Yasmina, fearing the scandal that my father was bound to unleash, let me know that she was clearing off by quietly pinching my arm. Had I less to lose than my sister by making a spectacle of myself among the neighbours, by escorting my father, who would not miss the chance to draw attention to us? I was a little vexed but I sacrificed myself. Besides, I was well known for having a bad memory and was very forgiving . . .

Ah, well.

'You won't mention it to anyone. Especially not Omar,' my father let slip in an almost normal voice.

Yasmina opened her mouth to say something, but changed her mind. I did likewise. What good was there in saying anything? My father was only worrying about the possession that he was afraid of losing for ever.

I slipped on a coat over my nightdress; I was afraid that my father would go out in his towel. But he went to put on an old suit reeking of mothballs.

Our eyes very soon got used to the moonlight and I longed for the blue darkness of the night. With bated breath, I concentrated my mind on my father's gibberish, his prayers addressed to his ancestors and his aunt. As I tried to untangle them, I was surprised to turn them around in my mother's favour.

We crossed the little road which was now deserted, although previously it had been lively until dawn with laughter, quarrels, card parties and draughts. Like two prowlers, we picked our way into Allouchi's garden and reached the door, our shoes weighed down by mud. My father stood aside and with graphic gestures asked me to knock on the door. I followed his orders. The nightingale stopped singing.

'Louder,' he whispered.

I clenched my fist, gathered my strength and thumped. At the first knock, the door opened with a deafening noise, on whirlwinds of shadows. A cat miaowed and jumped away. It only just missed me. Two shutters banged. We were being watched. But my father, not caring, asked me to go ahead of him and struck a match. A smell of patchouli hung in the air. The stubborn ticking of a watch tormented my nerves.

The match went out.

'Light it!' said my father, swearing, then wetting his fingers with saliva.

Trembling, cursing weddings, whether they were sham ones, love matches, marriages of convenience or of necessity, I managed to get to a wall. I groped, attacked by fears that had suddenly surged up from my childhood memories. At last my fingers brushed against a switch. I turned it on. No light came on. But why, O God?

'It's an abduction,' my father muttered. 'He won't find it easy to get rid of her,' he went on, as he lit a second match, only to blow it out at once.

In the twinkling of an eye, because, in spite of being as heavy as a hippopotamus, my father could be as nimble as a cat he was in the garden.

'An abduction! It's an abduction! I'll tell the authorities – *de jure* and *de facto*!'

12

Echoing my father, I managed to say:

'Omar's gone too.'

'Let him go!' shouted my father. 'Let him go! Since that's now a habit in this family!'

Shutters were closing. All around, people did not want to be called as witnesses.

'But he'd better not come back pregnant,' said my father, dropping his voice.

By a few tones.

Managing not to laugh, I followed on his heels, in a hurry to get within our own walls. To shut myself in and to forget. Forget the neighbours and their sarcastic remarks. Hide in there from the rest of the world and its horrors.

But my father stopped on the doorstep. And, as

though shouting Eureka! he snapped his fingers.

'Wait,' he said, just as I was disappearing from sight in the hall.

He had set his sights on the end of the road, where the woman engaged to be Nayla's chaperone lived.

No, Aziz Zeitoun! Pity! No! Enough!

But not a sound came out of my throat.

Aziz said:

'Let us go!'

I swallowed hard.

There we were, going down the road, and as we walked we frightened and chased the half-starved cats looking for scraps. There we were, having turned into puppets, amusing and enlivening the dull evenings of the street where Aziz the fisherman would soon stop creating the rain and the fine weather.

The woman took some time to answer us.

'Ah! It's you, *sidi* . . . excuse me, I was afraid . . . with all these tremors . . . don't you know.'

She played about with locks, fiddled with chains, and finally opened the door for us and greeted us as if we were an affliction. The flame of her candle flickered. In the shadow of her only room, her children were asleep in a row on mattresses thrown on the floor. A smell of frying clung to the walls. Sniffing noisily, my father looked around the room to inspect it. Did he hope to find my mother here? But she was nowhere to be seen. Not even a whiff of her strong perfume.

The woman offered us seats. We remained standing.

'So, my widow friend? What news?'

'Quiet, please, *sidi* Aziz. Please don't wake up my children,' she implored him, forgetting her widow-hood, which should make any woman demonstrate her humility, her shame...

Ah, well.

'Did they eat well, anyway? Was the fish fresh?'

'I'll pay you back...to the last sou...to the last sardine...' The woman shivered.

'That's not why I came!'

'I know, *sidi* Aziz, I know that...But, after the tremors, everyone left...'

'My widow friend, what are you talking about?'

'Whistling bullets...I'm talking about last night's tremors.'

'Don't talk rubbish,' my father cut in. 'What I want to know is what has happened to my wife, my wife whom you were supposed to look after...'

'I don't know...' she shivered.

'What do you mean, *I don't know*?' my father bellowed.

The children started to stir. One of them let out a groan.

'They took the train this morning, really early,' the woman admitted, looking anxiously around her.

My father raised his eyebrows and frowned.

'What train? Who took the train?'

'The two of them, Allouchi and Nayla... The train to the capital, I think...'

My father's jaw dropped in astonishment.

'I swear to you, *sidi* Aziz,' she went on, 'I couldn't stay any longer...I'd left my children on their own, and Allouchi was ordering me to go home, his wife, I mean Madame Nayla, was also asking me to leave... This morning, they seemed to be in a hurry...I have it from a neighbour, I've also heard...'

'What have you heard, my widow friend?'

'You know that people can be jealous and bad-mouthed in this neighbourhood,' she said, waving her hands in the air, as though she had suddenly got too hot.

'Go on,' hissed my father.

'It's said that Allouchi and Nayla...Oh, well, people say that it's a story that didn't start yesterday, that they were often seen together...What people thought was the jinnee's work is nothing but that of your...that is...'

In order to avoid uttering my mother's name, she suddenly put two fingers over her mouth and one hand on her chest, as if to convey to herself more than to us that she had got off lightly.

With his back against the door, my father seemed about to faint.

'Where were they seen?' he finally asked.

'You are not to be blamed, *sidi*,' the neighbour muttered, lowering her eyes. 'Sadly, no man can control a woman who's filled with the Devil...When they've caught that...'

'Where were they seen?' my father asked again,

puffing like a buffalo.

'I can't swear to anything, as God is my witness, I'm not going to burn in the slanderers' fire,' the woman whined.

'If you don't talk, I'll let you know about hell before your time!'

'With my own eyes, I saw them take a taxi, last winter, I think. Allouchi stopped the taxi, and she seemed to be very anxious, but didn't take any trouble to hide, as if we others weren't there. It took me a while to recognize her. Then I recognized her by her hair, her veil kept slipping off, she didn't seem to be used to having it on. Occasionally she wouldn't put it on again.'

She stopped talking.

Then, as if to pay my father a compliment, or comfort him, she added in a brusque, frightened voice:

'Her hair is so pretty, I couldn't forget it, she washed it so tenderly, in the old days, at the Turkish baths...'

'I'm sure she did,' my father grunted, in an absorbed sort of way.

I had a rough idea of the taxi story, which Omar knew as well, which would untangle these mistakes. It was only a question of time and certainly no business of mine.

Before he left, my father said:

'You don't owe me anything, my widow friend. But you'll be a witness when I've notified the authorities, *de jure* and *de facto*.'

13

He did not inform the legal authorities but he did ask
our religious advisor to come and see him, offered
him tea and cakes and told him about the disappearance of the adulterous pair.

'It is quite legitimate,' the Imam corrected him in a
neutral tone.

My father fidgeted but stayed calm.

'I'm telling you it is so,' he puffed, not taking his
eyes off the Imam.

'I married them,' the Imam reminded him.

'That's not what I'm talking about. I'm talking to
you about their liaison before this so-called marriage.'

'I understand,' said the Imam without batting an
eyelid. 'But I neither saw nor heard anything.'

'Well, listen to this now. Instead of being able to see

it, since they're no longer in the neighbourhood.'

'Their adultery, if there was adultery, is now expiated and absolved. God is forgiveness.'

'Don't tell me that you believed in this marriage,' my father retorted without losing his patience. Then he exclaimed: 'Abduction isn't part of the contract.'

'What contract are you talking about?'

'Our contract, as you know perfectly well.'

The Imam ignored the wink that Aziz the fisherman was giving him as a sign of complicity.

'I don't remember anything about a contract between us,' said the Imam, glancing furtively towards the door.

'Goodness me, Imam! Have you forgotten who I am?'

'Aziz Zeitoun the fisherman.'

'And benefactor!' my father cried waving a finger at him.

One way of bringing to order the person to whom he was speaking.

'May God take this seriously,' said the Imam.

He started to recite a couplet praising the greatness of Allah.

My father was delighted.

'Good,' he said.

Then he gave the man a friendly tap on the shoulder.

'Good,' he repeated. 'It's only a misunderstanding that's not important. Let's forget all that. Now it is a question of finding the mother of my children. We can't let this man carry off our women with impunity. Turn heaven and earth upside-down and find this traitor for me. Do it properly, Imam, and you'll be well rewarded for it.'

But the persuasion of Aziz the fisherman, like his admonishments, washed right over our man of law.

'Then we'll inform the authorities about the dangerous behaviour of this traitor,' my father went on.

'Youssef Allouchi is on holiday,' said the Imam. 'That's because he's got married. And, whatever you say, he hasn't disappeared, he went with Allah's blessing in his heart and marriage documents in good and proper form in his luggage.'

My father stared wide-eyed and, as though he had become suddenly deaf, he poked his finger in his ear and started to shake it vigorously.

'Wait a minute,' he said. 'I think we're not talking about the same thing, or at least not in the same way. I'm telling you again that my neighbour has abducted my wife.'

'You have a civil divorce, in front of witnesses, and a religious divorce, by your own actions,' the Imam stated impassively. 'Allouchi has insisted on arranging things properly, as they should be. He didn't want to run the risk, precisely, of being accused of adultery. Obviously, I could only approve of that. My role is to fit in with the wishes of believers. That's why we were witnesses,' he went on, looking again towards the door.

'Who were the witnesses, Imam?'

'Your son and I,' the Imam replied.

'Omar and you?'

Having been almost relaxed, sunk in an armchair, my father suddenly stood up straight and put his face close to the Imam's.

'Would you say again what you've just said,' he murmured like a rumble of thunder.

'I had warned you,' the Imam said, taking no notice of Aziz's familiar form of address. 'I had told you that things would be done according to the rules: witnesses, legal guardian, etcetera. The etcetera covered the "civil divorce". Those were my conditions. And if your neighbour repudiated his wife and you took her to be yours . . . The same conditions also.'

Every time he was vexed, my father started to shiver all over, bathed in his own sweat. For a short moment, he was quiet. He seemed to be sorting out his thoughts. Then with his mouth gaping and his eyes startled, he announced:

'We'd better start again from the beginning.'

'I'm really sorry,' the Imam grumbled. 'But those were my conditions . . .'

Thereupon, my father's strength and his 'king of the jungle' voice came back to him.

'You'll see, Imam, what I'll reduce your condition to! You'll see where your decisions will take you! You'll be lying in the gutter, Imam! I'll drown you! Believe me, it won't be Allouchi, that bullshitter, who'll pull you out!'

The Imam jumped up out of his chair. With one

hand, he gathered up his *gandoora* and with the other he picked up his skullcap, then before my father could react, the man had dashed off on his hairless, emaciated legs. Blessing us as he went out, he ran down the stairs like a goat.

My father rushed after him.

'How much did he pay you to plot this abduction with him? Maybe you were satisfied with a reading from the Qur'an, carefully avoiding: "Thou shall not touch thy neighbour's wife"?' he trumpeted.

But our father did not cross the threshold.

14

He did not go out of the house or even appear on the terrace any more. Locked in his bedroom, with his mind in a fog, he talked to his aunt, justifying capital punishment, torture and all forms of law, whether religious or not, monotheist or not, that condemned adultery of whatever kind, calling for traitors to be hanged and women of easy virtue to be stoned. In order to stock up on wine, to relieve his bladder or his stomach, he resigned himself to coming out of his den, with a heavy step, and his eyes reduced to slits. He walked in front of us without seeing us or hearing us. His aunt had now taken over his field of vision and his auditory faculties.

Our father was no longer himself; a stranger, a foreigner wandered around in our home, drank his wine, stayed in his room. So Aziz the fisherman let go of the reins and resigned. He was plunged head first in the depths of an abyss, his dignity in tatters. More than despair at knowing that his wife had fled or had been abducted — what did it matter? — Father suffered the pangs of dishonour, this ghastly fate reducing the strongest of males to nothing, to oblivion, forcing him to shave off his moustache, to swap his trousers for a *jebbah*, to shut himself in, as the company of men, real people, was taboo for him. These same men, who were our neighbours, curled their moustaches in an ostentatious manner and stuck out their chests and their chins. Despite that, they strengthened shutters and doors, thus barricading their wives in and any double-crossing whims these might have, as nobody was immune from you know what... What a woman wants... The wife of Aziz the fisherman, the daughter-in-law of Mahmoud Zeitoun, this orphan pulled out of the stream...

Whoever would have believed it?

Instead of alarming us, our father's defection, his madness, especially his withdrawal, made us very happy. From now on, provided it lasted, we were the masters of this ship. The twins stopped their enforced wanderings and looked after the two babies as if they had given birth to them. Between bottles and baby-powder sessions, they painted their portraits and those of their protégés congratulating themselves on the result, dancing pirouettes, clapping and resolving that they would soon reach the heights of fame. They gave themselves two years to complete a body of work. Then they would change the large ground-floor room leading on to the garden into a gallery. They would give it their own names, would send catalogues to the Ministry of Culture, invitations to the press, to VIPs and to friends . . .

I spent my evenings watching TV and smoking cigarettes stolen from my father's wardrobe. In the mornings, with a bitter taste in my mouth and the dull complexion of a dissipated person, toying with the plan to end my studies, I threw myself into the activities of daily life, my guts all knotted up, my legs like lead, veering off, steering a path towards boredom.

At the time, my only concerns were looking after the house and embroidery. In any case, the idea of having to spend my life using a typewriter had always made me sick. Besides, I immediately forgot what I learned: the school year was coming to an end and, unlike my friends who struck the keys as they chattered away or with their heads in the clouds, I could not type a line without staring at the keyboard. In short, my teachers despaired of my lack of dexterity and my faults. They stopped taking an interest in me. I was grateful to them for this.

Our fridge was getting empty, our meals were

becoming frugal, and when we invaded the stores laid down for the winter, tomatoes marinated in olive oil and salted dried fat, I finally gave up my typing course.

'You know best,' said Yasmina.

'I'm sure you're doing the right thing,' said Amina. 'The madder one is, the happier one can be.'

I made my plans, then carried them out to the letter. I telephoned my friends who were collecting sheets, tablecloths, dresses and caftans for their weddings, which were at least probable, if not imminent. I offered my services to them, cheaply, asking them at the same time to find customers for me; I placed an advertisement in the most widely read newspaper in the area, in which I stated the type of embroidery that I did, my rates, our telephone number and I fixed myself up in a bright corner of the living-room. I waited . . .

During this lethargy of my father's, we received a letter from Khadija posted from the capital, asking us to look after her son, telling us she was coming back, without saying when, or whether she had any news from her husband. To be honest, we didn't much care about her absence, nor our brother's. We had a lot to do and hardly any time to think about it.

Our neighbour's house was shut up and deserted, his garden was going to rack and ruin, his plants were

94

wizened, the nightingale had not sung for a long time, having left this place for the scents of other flowers, and our mother's adultery was no longer in any doubt...after all, what does a woman want?

Behind his bedroom door, my father wallowed in his wine, bogged down in his calculations, choking with remorse.

After all...

They did not reappear.

Had they not taken the train of their own free will?

Could he have guessed what she was doing alone in the house?

He should have padlocked the doors...

No, he should have locked himself in with her.

Were his children his own?

The Zeitouns did not have so many daughters. And if there were daughters, they were chaste, they did not stay out all night, did not let themselves be raped, did not reject their husbands, did not corrupt Imams, did not manipulate their sons. Isn't that right? Oh, my dear aunt! Oh, his aunt! What an insult!

If Youssef Allouchi had never got married, it was because he did not need to: his beloved was within reach. My father would rather say within beck and call, out of respect, but his aunt could translate this!

Oh, yes, he should have trusted his aunt's wisdom, he should have listened to her and never have repudiated his first wife, this poor cousin who was afflicted with ugliness and sterility, and who died of a broken heart. Also, maybe it was his fault that he had not had any children by his cousin.

Oh! my dear aunt, now turning in your grave, your last, damp home, that would explain the lineage of this traitor under my roof. Oh, yes, my dear aunt, the fresh complexion of this daughter of Satan turned my head. My naïve head. *Mea culpa*, Oh my dear aunt.

Oh, my dear aunt! Tell me that these tremors are only nightmares, and that the sky will be blue again.

15

The twins had nearly finished laying the table; Noria and Fouzia were revising their lessons for the end-of-year exams, I was embroidering, with my ear cocked towards the passage where the moanings of our outcast father were dying away.

'Yes, after all,' Amina dared to utter.

'Well, we've got to stop being ridiculous,' Yasmina replied. 'Mother ran away from shame. Omar, too, besides.'

Then:

'Who could imagine Mother getting up to such things? She hardly had time to do her housekeeping.'

'Did Allouchi, too, have to run away?' Amina retorted.

'He always used to disappear. We'll see him back soon.'

'I wouldn't mind being Allouchi's daughter...'

'Now look at us. We're the spitting image of Father.'

'Well, according to you, where might Mother be?' Amina enquired.

'Definitely in the village with her brother, for the period of three months, so that she can marry Father again. I'm sure that Allouchi kept his promise...'

'And the civil divorce?' said Amina.

'It's like the Imam said, to keep slander at bay.'

'My little finger tells me that Allouchi fell in love,' Amina insisted. 'Maybe he was already?' she added, looking sideways at her sister.

'Why do you always have to say really stupid things?' Yasmina asked. 'Especially in front of the little ones.'

'I–I'm not little.'

'Nor am I.'

'It's because I believe in love! I believe in it and I bow down before its experts.'

'So do-oo I.'

'So do I,' Fouzia echoed.

'That comes from the things you've been reading lately,' Yasmina sighed.

'I've read holy books too, which our holy sister-in-law would condone and praise. Did you know, for example, that a woman who's unhappy in her marriage enjoys the pleasures of love in the beyond? Another life, more children? It's written in black and white in the Holy Book.'

'Are we going to get more brothers and sisters?' Fouzia asked.

Staring, Noria fiddled with her exercise book.

'Who knows?' asked Amina.

'We'll have nothing of the kind! She'll end up by poisoning your minds!' Yasmina shouted.

Then, to me:

'You could tell her to shut her trap instead of grinning like that.'

Noria closed her exercise book, got up and clenched her fists. And like a demonstrator protesting in support of preserving home life, dodging the words that would not cling to her tongue, she chanted:

'Mother's not dead! Father's behind the door! Mother's going to come back! With Father she will frolic!'

When she had finished chanting, Noria tidied her bits and pieces and stated that she was going to bed without any supper. Fouzia did likewise. That's how they put an end to the discord between the twins.

'It's not worth taking it like that,' Amina said, catching them in the passage. 'I only meant that Mother doesn't need to wait for another life before she can have some sort of compensation.'

That evening, our mother's absence weighed very heavily on us and for quite some time we no longer mentioned her name.

16

At the end of the month, some of my father's employees came to ask about their boss's health, their future and their wages. We received them on the doorstep. Not knowing what to say, we asked them to call again. Which they did the next day.

However, none of us dared to disturb our father in his meditations. As my mother had still not come home – and in fact we were no longer expecting her to return – we were afraid to take the lion out of his cage and thus put an end to the peacefulness of our new life.

'A letter!' Amina exclaimed. 'Write a letter to them. Pretend that it's from Father.'

Being illiterate in both languages, as he said himself, my father used to solicit our help in order to write a letter of protest to the revenue or the water company, which he would then show to my mother – as she had been allowed to have a few years' schooling – before he signed it, writing his own name in big wobbly capital letters which filled him with pride. He would have been a famous surgeon, or an astronaut flying across the heavens, he would assert, if he had been given the chance of going to school.

'It's money they want, not words,' Yasmina retorted.

'In the letter, he'll give them everything!'

'You're out of your mind!'

'He'll give them everything. Temporarily, until Omar comes back,' Amina explained. 'In any case, we've no choice. It's either that or we rouse Father.'

So we drafted a letter in which my father announced that he was retiring, which he should have done a few years earlier. (We did not know his age, his civil papers stated, 'Presumed date of birth...' but he was around sixty.)

For the moment, maybe permanently, the letter stated, he was delegating the management of his trawlers to his dear and devoted staff: sale of the produce, managing the equipment, sharing the profits among the staff... Thus we rebuilt the business of Aziz the fisherman into a self-managing cooperative and we wished a fair wind and great success to the management committee. We asked for only one thing (more to add to the credibility of the gift than to please our taste, as we were rather fonder of red meat, a rarity in our house): if there was a good catch, the family would appreciate a crate of red mullet or king prawns.

Yasmina made a perfect imitation of the donor's signature, over which she delicately applied the stamp with the firm's seal.

The staff, when we gave them the letter, looked at us sceptically. But not for too long. Once they had the gift in their hands, they remembered their boss's misfortunes, which were continuing to provide fodder – as we knew, but at present it rolled off us like water off a duck's back – for the cafés in the neighbourhood and in the harbour. Aziz the fisherman was finally humiliated, Aziz the fisherman was bathed in disgrace... Allah's mercy was certainly boundless, they were going to make good use of this gift from heaven. Thank you. A thousand thanks. They would never forget him.

We did not see my father's staff again. Nor any crates of fish. But we lived in peace. It was as though the earth was no longer shaking.

I put more advertisements in the newspaper and every day I had double the number of customers. I used to let them in when my father was taking care to sleep off his wine, I gave them tea and biscuits baked by the twins, who were getting on well with the cooking.

In the light in the living-room, with a smell of patchouli, dressed in red, my hair hanging loose on my shoulders, I discussed matters, arguing about delivery times, suggesting models, advising on thread and fabric, negotiating prices... And money started to come in again. Our fridge was always full of meat, cheese, Coca-Cola and top-price kiwis. Thanks to nappies and imported milk, Zanouba and Mahmoud no longer had red bottoms or diarrhoea. The twins were getting keener and keener on cooking, to the detriment of their artistic careers, and cooked up dishes that we polished off, licking our fingers. We were getting noticeably fatter. Even our father had given up ignoring the plate that we left in front of his door. Fouzia and Noria went shopping as though to a dance. At the bottom of the shopping basket, there was always a bottle of patchouli, a scarf or undergarment in my mother's favourite colours, which they then lovingly hid in their cupboard. Sometimes before they went to bed, they checked to see if the presents for their mother were still there.

17

One day, Noria and Fouzia came back early from school. Noria lisped incomprehensible words, then stopped to go and look for honey.

'Thi-is will help me to ex-x-plain,' she said as she opened the jar.

She was as white as her school blouse.

But the honey was no help.

'Ear-earthquakes . . . T-tremors.'

That was all.

Frightened by the curse that lay on her voice, none the less Fouzia picked up the story. She launched into a description of the tremor which had destroyed the nursery beside their school.

'There were arms, legs everywhere, everywhere,' she went on, her cheeks changing from red to ashen.

'I even saw fingers stuck to a piece of wall that fell down from the front of the building. I picked them up and gave them to the headmaster, who was looking for his family like a madman. He took the fingers, counted them, and there was one missing, probably the thumb, but he said that didn't matter. He was stroking them as he wailed. He shivered as he waited for the ambulance, then suddenly he kissed them gently with his lips, and he couldn't stop saying that I was a good girl. When his eyes were no longer clouded by tears, he fell silent and suddenly the veins in his neck grew larger and turned blue, then his eyes popped out of his head. He threw the fingers in my face, shouting that he didn't need a woman's fingers. I peered closely at them and the nails were painted with red, bright red nail polish...I wonder how I didn't see all this red...'

'That's enough!' Yasmina spat out.

'And the rest? Don't you want the rest? Does nobody want the rest of the story?'

'Go on,' said Amina, vigorously grabbing her twin's hand.

'No! No! No!' Yasmina shouted again, releasing herself from Amina's grip.

'Don't get into such a state,' said Fouzia. 'It was God's wish. My teacher, when she found her little daughter, said...My teacher, by the way, had a four-year-old daughter in this nursery. Well, my teacher said that, despite everything, one shouldn't be angry with God and she wasn't even crying. That's life, that's life, she was saying over and over to everybody, but nobody really listened to her because everybody had something to say or repeat.'

Noria hiccuped, stifled a burp, rolled her eyes as if to make an excuse.

'Isn't that true?' Fouzia went on, looking at Noria.

The latter gave her answer by rolling her eyes again.

Suddenly, Yasmina started to talk like our father, in a deep cavernous voice:

'Because He has kept us out of heaven, we can't really be angry with Him. We must ask Adam and Eve to account for themselves. More Eve than Adam, in fact. But when He makes mothers of us without our asking, when He makes Mother and Omar disappear on the same day, when He makes the earth shake and blow up nurseries, when He takes away reasoning powers from adults and even children, when He doesn't help a man to find fingers, one can only be angry with Him!'

Amina anxiously raised an eyebrow.

'Are you all right?' she asked her quietly.

'Oh, I know,' said Yasmina, in a slightly calmer voice. 'I know well it's no time for blasphemy.'

'No, it's not the time,' Amina replied. 'Also, why be angry with this woman who came out of her man's ribs?'

'Was sh–she a cutlet?' said Noria.

'That's enough,' Fouzia mumbled as she ran off to the toilet, where she was noisily sick.

'It's Fouzia who's not well,' said Yasmina.

Then each of us in turn, each in our own rhythm, threw ourselves over the wash-basin to bring up our lunch.

18

Life was going swimmingly again, when our father left his lair, sober and just like his old self. Almost. The stock of wine was exhausted without our having noticed. If we had noticed it, none of us would have agreed to go and buy some, nor would we have known how to do this: my father ordered his wine by the barrel. And what rash wine merchant would have served a woman? Even in the capital, that was not done any more.

I had spent a great deal of time during the night on an embroidery order, a *saroual* belt, in fine gold–thread embroidery; my eyes were burning and the shooting pain which had been there for some days made my back really stiff. Each step and each movement scrunched up my body like an electric shock. That morning, I should have stayed in bed.

The smell of coffee had pleasantly aroused my taste-buds; would the twins have made it, those girls who, since freedom of choice had come into our home, only made tea?

When I went into the kitchen, he was standing there, with his bottom leaning on the edge of the sink; he was drinking coffee. Between gulps, he stared first at the inside of his cup and then at the groceries piled on the table. He could believe neither his eyes nor his nose. Seeing me there, and without looking at me, he said:

'Well done.'

Then he slowly fingered the edge of the cup. As though he were contemplating an unprecedented catastrophe. Then I had only one wish: to retrace my steps, get back to my room and double-lock my door. But lead ran down my legs and filled my feet.

'Well done,' he said once more. 'First of all you make your mother vanish, then you live off my ruin.'

'I ... It's the embroidery ...'

Useless. Even if he had been in his right mind, my father would never have believed me.

'A widower and ruined before time. Well done. A thousand bravos,' he repeated, his eyes on the leg of lamb.

While he redoubled his lamentations and praises, I thought again about the forgery, that letter where we had made him hand over his business to his staff. Wincing, I murmured:

'Thank you.'

But he heard it.

'She tramples on my dignity and she answers me,' he growled.

He pounced on me. He grabbed me by the hair. Then he pulled it. With all his strength. First upwards. Then downwards. Until my knees were bent.

'She is defying me! This bigot of an Imam is defying me! Allouchi is defying me! My son has betrayed me. They are eating out of my hands and they are defying me, they are eating out of my hands and they betray me,' he said, the words disjointed, each syllable emphasized.

All of a sudden, he let go. I lost my balance and fell over. My face hit the cold tiles. I did not like milk and never drank it, so my teeth shattered like glass. I could do nothing about it and what mattered for the moment was to save my skin.

While he was meticulously removing the tuft of hair that was stuck between his fingers, shouting, Ah! and, Oh ! with pleasure, I crawled under the table, clearing an escape route between the chairs. But he caught me, grabbed my hair again and started to drag me all around the house.

'Why? What have I done? What is it I have done?'

My sisters were awakened by my shouting. The twins called for help, shouted themselves hoarse, stirring up the neighbourhood. In vain. Outside, men hurried on, laughing nervously; women opened their shutters, warding off ill fortune by spitting into their bosom, and the more sensitive ones shed a tear.

'Poor creatures, poor orphans.'

'That's how his house must be purified.'

'Like mother, like daughters.'

'That will only do those women good.'

'May He protect us from evil.'

Etcetera. Etcetera.

Noria and Fouzia ran out into the street, begging the neighbours to call the police, the fire brigade or the hospital. The men continued to hurry past. But they were laughing less.

'The police and the fire brigade have better things to do.'

'The earth tremors are getting stronger and stronger.'

'There's no more room in the morgues.'

In short, nobody moved.

Throughout this time, my father, with my hair in his iron grip once more, was gloating in dragging me around his well-appointed, well-built house. While my body, my head, my whole carcass was banging against the walls. While my blood was dripping down my face, and staining the floor. While my sisters were howling as she-wolves howl at the time of death. While the babies were crying themselves into a state of exhaustion. While my creator accused me sometimes of being a mother who had killed her baby, and sometimes of being a child who had killed her mother. While the words left his mouth and reached my nerve cells on the path of a frantic escape. While

111

these same words took shape and knocked my eyeballs sideways. While the pain anaesthetized me, while my feet froze with the coldness of Siberia. While the pain courted me and seduced me, memories which had been sealed up in the very depths of my mind broke free, then ran off at a dizzy speed, to get away from the crazy pain. And at the same speed I knew why I was a runaway, a sly person, a liar and a sham. I knew why my mother had never breast-fed her youngest child and why she had abandoned her. I knew why the angels' wrath had not roared down on her and Zanouba had been spared the drain in the laundry, Zanouba or Manouba having been born as strong as a bear, even though she was very premature.

PART THREE

PART THREE

19

She has been scalped. Literally...Oh, God! How horrible! How can anyone attract assaults in that way? Provoke them? Well, one must not go out like that. A woman is never safe. And then women are not made for hanging about the streets...Her father? Over a leg of lamb? It's true that meat is very dear, but all the same, what a fate! O Thou who sees everything, who hears everything, protect our children! The poor little girl. Nearly a year ago, she was in the same ward. That time, flayed alive and her virginity torn to shreds...How can one shatter the life of a child?...One has to say that it's a miracle, or that she is absolutely determined to live. Some people commit suicide for less...

A coma? Who knows? A cranial traumatism? Clinically dead? Maybe it's only a kind of blackout.

That can last a very long time. We must wait till the scanner is fixed and bring her back here – if she's still in the land of the living by then. Stitches and bandages. That is all we can do. Alas! We've got no beds. Not even a pillow. A great many patients, these days, with torn membranes, pitted skin, necks to be stitched up, hands to be mended . . . Anyway, we mustn't complain; besides, elsewhere they've no respite. Night and day. Oh, yes, the tremors are so severe . . . Even Zafiroun Fateh was overwhelmed, in fact he died of it.

After stitching her up, take her home. Then wait. Make her drink sweet water. As good as glucose serum. Rinse her mouth with salt water; that heals the gums really well, better than sidi-saint medicine. Oh, yes, my dears, you'll have to get on with it. If she doesn't wake up within a week . . . forget it. Besides, in view of the state she's in, it would be better for her.

Forget me? Don't think about it. Am I not the pillar of the family? Am I not made in the image of the fish and the bull who hold up the earth? It would be fatal to supplant me.

Collapse.

In an incandescent light, I recognized the pale colours of my bedroom, the flowery curtains, the wallpaper with big tulips, and the four pairs of eyes that were staring at me, the four mouths that were breathing inexpressible sighs.

'He actually dislocated your jaw,' Amina said, half-smiling.

'I'd really like to see what's under that bandage,' Fouzia puffed.

'You have been in a big sleep and we had a... terrible fright,' Yasmina added.

'Days in the pickle,' said Fouzia.

'Da-ays without mo-ney.'

'In any case, we missed you.'

Neither the blood, nor the shouting, nor my sudden silence had frightened our father. But when he saw that there was no more than one strand of hair left on my scalp, as Amina said, he had stopped.

'He thought you were dead,' Yasmina went on.

'I think he found there was nothing left for him to pull out,' said Amina, giving me a first spoonful of consommé.

'Maybe he was going to ca-carry on by attacking us?' Noria shivered, rolling up her eyes till her eyelashes touched her eyebrows.

Yasmina tried to change the subject.

'For a while now, she has taken a sacred delight in being afraid,' she said. 'She has nightmares. We can't sleep any more because of her shouting. She doesn't want to tie herself to the bed any more. We've ended up spending our nights catching her in the garden or on the street corner...'

A vain attempt.

'He left you alone because the telephone rang,' Amina went on.

'The telephone was later,' said Fouzia.

Then she started to tell the story.

'Have you dug up Allouchi's new address?' our father was saying to the person on the telephone, his hands still covered with my blood. 'I wish you luck...That's too bad, as I need money too...I've just been ruined...As I said, ruined, all my money went on feeding my daughters, who, as you must know, are not my daughters...But my wife is dead, sir...No, that was not a slip of the tongue. I never make slips of the tongue...I'm Aziz the fisherman, you must never forget that...Only do you know that a woman who was mistreated by her husband finds happiness in heaven? Yes, sir, and you must know this, my wife was unhappy with her husband...This traitor Youssef Allouchi, this son of a Christian, maybe even of a Jew, had, however, promised to look after her...Oh, yes, oh, yes. Thou shalt not offer thy wife to thy neighbour. I know all that. Be that as it may, at the same time as you are busy trying to rob me, you are definitely the accomplice of my neighbour's progeny; sadly I have no way of proving this, my wife is coddling her new children...'

At that moment, somebody knocked at the door, banging loudly. While my sisters were holding their breath, were praying, hoping for a miracle, my father hung up and went to open the door. Muffled voices came up from downstairs. There were a great many of them, talking hurriedly and nervously. Then, Fouzia went on, greedy for words, our father's voice cried out:

'Carry what? Who? My boats are made for fishing and not for what you say. It's a plot! It's a frame-up! Allouchi and his daughters want to get the better of me! So ask your neighbours to tell you about the dirty tricks that have been played on me! I can't sleep any more! I can't eat any more! I'm as empty as a leather bottle.'

A few more, nearly audible, murmurs, but Fouzia had taken in nothing. And again our father's voice, louder and louder:

'But it's the traitor living across the road that must be taken away. He's the one who knows how to read and write, who drafts – how do you say that? Suservive? Subversive – documents, of course. I don't even know what that means, literary Arabic's not my thing, you know...But I can tell you that I don't do that, don't do anything susertive. Go and see my neighbour's place. Even if he marries our wives according to the law of temporal marriage, and if one of them catches his attention, that is, I mean, if she pleases him, he has no trouble in bribing the Imams, and even the sons, in order to register their marriage. Upon my word, he thinks he's the Emir Saud! He throws himself on to our wives any old how, precisely because he's impotent. When he wants to forget about his problem, my neighbour takes out his gun, saying it's for the ceremony, dada dada...In fact he fires his shots in order to give the lie about what is being said about him, what is known about him. But these poor women don't last and give up the ghost. My good friends, I'm only a shipowner, I'm the most famous in the harbour, certainly, but only a shipowner, one of the most generous. Nothing else, certainly not an arms dealer. In fact, I don't like weapons. So to claim that my boats are hiding-places...Someone has just telephoned me who knows where the real guilty party has gone to ground. Oh, yes, my dear sirs, unlike me, Youssef Allouchi is in hiding. Unlike me, his mind is not at rest! It's not as if I have ever abandoned my children in someone else's house! I have never used my bastards in order to rob my neighbours! Ask them, they'll tell you. They miss nothing...Around here, no secret is safe. Oh, no, he didn't give me Allouchi's address, nor his own, either. Now that I think about it, he didn't even leave his name. He wanted money. A colossal amount that I haven't got. A sort of ransom to give me back my wife, may God have mercy on her soul. But my neighbour's daughters have spent every penny. In fact, they've robbed me. They're the ones who should be taken away. Not me. They and their father. They're the ones who should be thrown into your gaols...So even if I knew that address, I wouldn't give it to you...We're not informers, we Zeitouns. Our name has never been associated with a renegade, or an informer. No, indeed!'

Then in a thundering, broken voice:

'Not me! Not me! I'm an honest citizen! Neither a renegade nor an informer! I like red wine and I've enjoyed it, which is the most illegal thing of all! My wine barrels come from monasteries, I tell you! I never go to the mosque! Ransack my house! Indict me! Take all the time you want, I give you permission. Really happily. You'll see that I haven't got a single prayer-mat, or the smallest skullcap. I don't know how to turn myself towards the Kaaba, for God's sake!'

His outburst drowned the noise in the street, then car doors banged and our father's voice faded away.

'There you are, we don't even know where he is,' said Amina.

'It's because of that silly letter,' said Yasmina.

'The damage is done, now. We're not going to start blaming anyone again,' was Amina's retort.

'In any case, Father's gone mad. Really mad. In this neighbourhood, people talk about nothing else,' said Fouzia.

'They say that he was be-wi-witched by Mother, that she made him eat donkey's brain. It's unbearable,' Noria joined in.

'Everybody's talking about the woman who dared to repudiate her husband,' Fouzia continued.

'It's the story of Mo-ther.'

'Alas, love will always be under suspicion,' Amina puffed.

'Our family carries on breaking up,' said Yasmina.

Amina looked at her as if she had never heard anything so absurd.

'These days what family is still together? Besides, the earthquakes are still going on. And all the volcanoes are erupting. The lava has engulfed whole villages.'

'They say that Mother and Allouchi are living in the desert, where there are no tremors or volcanoes. Only oil. They even say that Mother's expecting a baby,' Fouzia asserted.

'They say anything they like,' Yasmina moaned.

'You can't be sure about that,' said Amina. 'My little finger...'

'That's enough,' Yasmina cut in.

'Tha-at's enough,' I said.

I was stammering.

'But you're sta-ammering!' Noria shouted.

'You've only got little tiny stubs left for your front teeth,' said Fouzia, making a face at me.

'Stumps,' Noria grimaced in turn.

'I'd like a mirror,' I said.

Silence. Head-shaking. Nail-biting. Exchanging of looks. General agitation. A new attempt at changing the subject. It did not bode well at all.

I insisted on it.

'Please,' I lisped, my tongue avoiding the empty space in my gums.

Amina shrugged her shoulders and agreed to bring one.

'You might as well admire yourself in the mirror immediately,' she said.

'So-o, we won't say any more about it.'

The stitches on my skull, which had been sewn in a hurry, with a thick thread and needle, were pulling so that my nose was turned up; my eyes were slits; my eyebrows and the corners of my mouth slanted upwards. Also, I had a petrified look as if in a state of permanent amazement, crossed with an imperceptible smirk.

'You must lose something each time,' Amina moaned.

Yasmina gave her an admonitory look, then breathed a deep sigh. I smiled as I watched my sisters; now they were not behaving like my sisters. Without saying a word, I started to remove the bandage which was dripping blood on to my head. As the cloth was gradually unwound, my sisters bit their lips or the inside of their mouths, and their nostrils quivered with fear.

My bare head had the expected effect; with one voice, they uttered ahs and ohs of disgust. Two blistered, oozing, zigzag lines, obviously indelible, completed the ugly scene.

'First the memory, then the face,' I said.

'You can say so,' murmured the horrified and worried Amina.

But immediately, as if waking up, she went on:

'If you can talk about the memory, that's because you remember.'

'Oh, yes,' I said.

With vigorous movements, Yasmina started to paint my head with iodine.

'Oh, yes?' she said, incredulously.

'I hadn't really forgotten.'

"Nor I,' said Noria.

'Nor I either,' Fouzia joined in. 'But as I wasn't

allowed to speak, I couldn't say anything to you. Will you forgive me, my dear sister?'

'Becau-ause of the way I talk, you wouldn't have understood very much. Will you for-rrgive me, too?'

'Of c-course,' I said.

As one, we glanced at Zanouba, who was crossing the room on all fours, babbling and calling the twins 'Mama'. Then we smiled when Mahmoud shouted out in protest, jealous of his cousin's agility.

20

A few days later, while Noria and Fouzia were out shopping in the market, Yasmina said to me:

'Do you remember everything ?'

'Yes . . . Apart from a few details. Maybe.'

'So Father hit you in the right place,' said Amina. Then:

'Do you want the details in order or out of order?'

'Do you really want us to talk about it?' asked Yasmina, with her typical delicacy.

'Yes.'

'Father has fixed what the others and he himself had wrecked,' said Amina.

'All the same, he went too far when he said you were dead.' Yasmina smiled. 'Just like that, without blinking an eyelid. That doesn't mean you weren't within an ace of convincing him.'

'He would have preferred to see you dead rather than tarnished. So he hit you. It has to be said that he didn't have time to disfigure you, like over the leg of lamb. He had lost consciousness before that. And Mother was there.'

'Are you sure you want to talk about it?' Yasmina asked again.

'Yes!'

'Very well,' she said.

But she did not say a word.

It was Amina who carried on:

'When you began to put on weight, Mother put you in a corset and she began to wear a cushion under her dress. Then she would only sleep in your room, pretending that she couldn't bear to be pregnant... Do you remember that?'

'Vaguely,' I answered.

'I would never have believed that Mother would do such a thing,' Yasmina murmured.

She began to raise her eyebrow slowly, as if she were trying to drive back an unhappy memory. Or remorse. She said:

'She loved us, but she didn't know how to show it. That's normal when one hasn't had a mother.'

'Well done for working that out,' said Amina. 'And if we go on, we must conclude that we won't be able to show our love for our children either, since Mother didn't teach us how.'

She paused, then began again straightaway:

'You're right, one has to learn how to love. In any case, it needs practice. Those stories of maternal instinct only apply to animals.'

Then, suddenly, as she looked at me: 'Your example is proof of it.'

I could not help clearing my throat.

'I'm so sorry,' said Yasmina, waving her arms as a sign of helplessness.

'It doesn't matter,' I said. 'It means nothing to me.'

We heard the flies buzzing, also Zanouba gurgling in her own corner. Yasmina broke the silence and did not let her twin get another word in.

'Really Mother was afraid of being repudiated. She wasn't eating any more. Father put her attitude and her ill-health down to a pregnant woman's whims... After all her miscarriages, he was hoping for a second son. His village saint had told him about that in a dream. You know the song... In any case, she would have shone in his eyes. In fact, she disobeyed Father who wanted you to have an abortion. He didn't believe in violence, but, to save face, he said that the Mufti of Bosnia had approved of abortion for women who... anyway... you know...'

'He organized everything,' she went on. 'The doctor, the certificates of unfitness, as if you had heart trouble. But Omar was against it, strongly against it. He wanted you to live in the village, with the baby. Then Mother talked about a so-called fall down the stairs, and she locked you in the laundry. Father and Omar swallowed this story. Then Omar thought that you had done it on purpose – falling downstairs, that is. He will always blame you...even though he persisted in finding the culprits. How can anyone recognize beings who have come up from the bowels of the earth? How does one tell aliens apart... would you know them, yourself?'

It was Amina's turn to interrupt her sister.

'That's enough,' she said.

'Later,' Yasmina continued, not to be deflected, 'Zanouba was born as strong as a...'

'That's enough,' I said in turn.

21

The heat made the air as heavy as lead, it dilated it, made the sky turn yellow, driving back the salutary showers, bringing sandstorms, drying up the breath, dulling movements and minds, setting off the babies' exhausted cries.

However, summer was drawing to a close.

My head was sweating under the bandage and, when the perspiration dried, the itching was unbearable. I took off the bandage then and did not put it on again. From that time on, my clients only looked at me secretly. Touching wood surreptitiously – discreetly brushing against the old oak table on which the petits fours, the Ceylon tea and American cigarettes for smokers had pride of place – they had a problem hiding their repugnance. While their brows were beaded with embarrassment, they then overdid their act of putting on compassion. It also happened that they fought off a violent and irrepressible need to laugh. I would wait and hope for these moments.

In order to put my awkward clients at ease, I would make up an anecdote, and as the slightest funny story gave them an excuse for laughing, the most harmless story, with the least humour, became the escape route which freed both them and me.

Ah, well.

Zanouba and Mahmoud had not got used to my new appearance either. When I came near them, they became petrified, then gave a loud, shrill cry; my sisters nicknamed me *Tales from the Crypt*, their favourite TV series. In their desire to comfort me, they discussed the miracles of cosmetic surgery and implants, chose and noted down names and addresses, sent a great many letters to hospitals, charitable institutions, non-governmental organizations, elected representatives and various bigwigs from abroad... And they watched out for the postman.

'They'll reply and they'll agree to treat you,' they would say. 'Your journey will be organized in a flash, visa and everything. Your head will be in the care of Professors X or Y, or the two of them, and will be all fixed up in two ticks,' they went on.

Faced with my doubtful if not indifferent expression, they talked about an easy job, child's play, as it would have nothing to do with my face... Isn't that right, Yasmina? They would only need to undo the stitching on the scalp, then sew it up again skilfully, using the right stuff. Isn't that right, Amina?

'The latest thing!' they yelped in unison.

Were they not big-hearted, with justice in their blood, descendants of Lalla Mariam, the heirs of the Messiah?

In order to stop the euphoria of my younger sisters, who had turned into my offspring – I do not know how or why, by what method – I agreed, knowing that their plans were unworkable as well as Utopian.

I would wear a wig or, failing that, would wear a veil. What did I have to hide other than disgrace? I would cover my face completely, and would adopt, as much as I could, the Afghan cowl; I would see the world through holes and the world would not see me. What was wearing a veil compared with violent, unpredictable earthquakes, which shook the earth and tore it apart, catching unawares those who were passing, swallowing them up without warning? Why should I worry about people's horrified looks when volcanoes roared, turned red, vomited, spewing lava, burying those who lived nearby, snapping short their lives without any compunction?

After thinking about it, I would not wear a veil at all. In broad daylight I would display my features, which were artificially pulled upwards, my perpetual astonishment, my toothless, enforced giggle and my ugly scars. That would show other people – who exactly would it show? – or it would not show them. What does it matter? I would think about that later on. For the time being, the change in my face, however repugnant, hardly upset me at all. In any case, I did not go out as I had no time, and neither needed nor wished to do so. Like a mother, from now on my days would be spent between four walls. Besides, I was always happy thus.

The headaches gave me no respite, fever took me by surprise at any time of the day or night; my sleep was filled with visions of terror; from the depths of my subconscious, or from a place which was still further back in my brain, no doubt unknown to the specialists, sickening, revolting people appeared suddenly. Like that nurse with the comforting, serene smile, who bandaged my wounds She muttered a few words with rounded lips. Words that I could not understand but which seemed to hold the promise and guarantee that I would be healed. Then, very gently indeed, she let her fingers run through my hair, and stroked my cheeks. She always seemed to have the familiar face of a forgotten friend, sometimes it was Khadija's at the time when she had not yet become my sister-in-law, but her body was abnormally large, with long, disjointed limbs that were out of proportion. And she would lay me down on my back, gently, always smiling. Then, suddenly, a strange expression would distort her features, her face would be stripped of its skin, tufts of hair, like sideburns, would grow on her cheeks... Then she would have no resemblance to anything that could have been the Lord's work.

When I averted my eyes from this abominable apparition, she would start to recite in a strange language. Gradually I recognized the verses from the Qur'an which were recited to children to calm them down after a nightmare. While a feeling of security came over me, the woman would begin to utter the Fatiha. In one go and in reverse. Having finished this ceremony, she would throw herself upon me, press her lips on top of mine, would root in my mouth with her tongue, would hold me tight, so that my limbs were immobilized. That's when I felt against my lower abdomen the hardness of a penis, as long as a club. My cries only succeeded in irritating the woman-man, if I may call it that, to intensify her loud groans and she would penetrate me with the strength of a giant.

When I was nearly fainting, she withdrew, hairy and breathless, with a wicked, fixed grin emphasizing her ugliness. Then other women-men, just like the first, would carry on where the last one left off. In turn and *ab irato*.

I struggled in vain against the memory of these dreams; my mind was still confused by them and my body was drained. Then the nights began to nibble away at my days and ended up by devouring them. As soon as the sun went down, I sank into acute anxiety and fear held me in a state of high fever. Trembling all over, gnashing my teeth, wrapped in a blanket, tottering, I turned round and round. What to do, O God, to put an end to this coldness that I alone felt? In order to defy it, I would take ice-cold showers, without caring about making the wounds on my head, which would not heal, so much worse.

From that time on it was out of the question to sleep, to meet those beings – I had reached the stage of missing the ghouls, the gnomes, who not very long ago had agitated my childhood dreams; I had reached the stage of missing my father's treatment, his prohibitions, his criticism, his law which had driven the horrors of this world back into the depths of my being, to the extent of blanking out the memory of some faces; his law which frightened me until my memory stopped working. Those faces which now passed through my nights were of another calibre. They were more sinister than sordidness, more real than reality. For a long time I restrained myself from telling anybody about these strange visits. And even if I had wanted to talk about them, I could not have found the words.

To stop sleeping was the only way to escape from them.

I would escape from them; I swore it.

At the beginning of this self-imposed insomnia, Amina insisted on keeping me company. Fighting the heaviness of her eyelids, my sister would read to me, her favourite book being a thick one whose story, according to her, gave her a feeling of *déjà vu.*

'Doesn't this mean anything to you?' she would ask.

Amina persisted; however we had agreed to stop speculating on the love affair – which was still unconfirmed – of our mother and her husband. I looked at my sister reproachfully and heavily, then I looked down at my handiwork.

'That's the story that I'd like to live out,' she went on, pretending to finish off. 'Not you?'

Faced with my silence, she raised her eyebrows with a sad face and started describing again Ariadne's curved eyebrows, long legs and the money which was spent foolishly on pleasing her Lord... When the heroine ran away, the husband sank into depression, and my sister could not help pausing in a silence that was filled with hidden meanings. Then she started asking me more questions, peered at me, stared at me. In the hope of infecting me with her languor, she watched out for my sighs of delight. But I stayed as still as a stone. Then she would close the book, hold it tight to her chest, give me a little peck on my forehead and go to bed, advising me to do the same.

I did not know then that my sister was in love. I was certainly a very bad mother.

Later on at night, when my work fell out of my hands, I would stare at the TV. Until I was sick of it. And even if sleep wanted to take me away with it, it could never possess me. I never fell asleep, the voices from the screen pulling me out of slumber and reviving my mind.

22

On account of my aches and pains and the lack of sleep – I only dozed off at the first light of dawn, with the curtains open and the light hitting my eyelids – I moved about with difficulty, tottering like an old woman. My sight was getting steadily worse and it took longer and longer for the fog clouding my eyes to clear. But nothing could stop me getting back to work, everything pushed me towards it. I stored up the little bit of strength I had left and saved it so as to let it come out whenever I seized my tambour frame.

So I settled down to work, day and night, night and day, obstinately to protect my family from poverty and pity, to sustain the members of my family who, by my own fault – oh, yes, by my own fault: I shall explain this later on, if I have the chance – were now insecure, left to their own devices, and to me. Luckily, my clients became more and more extravagant, they became bourgeois, the number of parties increased like so many acts of survival, or of ʻresistance, or immortality. How should I know?

In order to stay awake, I got into the habit of talking to myself.

One night, as my mind was straying into endless musing about the future of my family and the world, I felt a presence. A real one.

Just one breath had warmed my neck then had run down my arms; I was overwhelmed by a feeling of well-being. I turned around slowly and he was there in front of me. I saw him. This was not a product of my imagination.

No.

It was a man.

In flesh and blood.

Tall and good-looking.

A white cotton-like beard, thick and wavy, covered his torso and flowed down to his waist; his hands were soft, shining with kindness, his fingers were thin; his nails were immaculate. In spite of his great age, there were no brown patches on his skin. His face, too, was light, shining, unwrinkled; his eyes were a clear as Brazilian emeralds in which one could see one's reflection.

He stood there, with his arms crossed over his beard, his torso erect, his shoulders hinting at an inhuman or too-human suppleness.

He smiled.

What am I saying?

Light poured from him and the room was filled with a silky, satin light with incredibly soft pastel glints.

Who sent him? Why was he here?

(I did not ask any questions; I had a feeling that I knew the answers.)

What region did he come from?

He was not from anywhere local, or even from our region: his style, the quality of his clothes, which were white with pink and blue shades – everything, in fact, indicated that he was not from our own area.

What language did he speak? Did he speak more than one? Did he speak at all?

He said nothing, not at the beginning. He greeted me by inclining his head, a graceful bow. If I had lost my reason, I would have said that he was the Angel Gabriel, or his counterpart, who had come to offer me a career as a prophetess. But I was completely *compos mentis*, and the desert was a long way off.

He was a wise man, or some such; in any case, he had the greatness of one, I knew that straight away, and I was not afraid of him for one moment. Every night he came back. He would come just after the stroke of midnight. How? By which entrance? I had no interest in finding out (did I know?), the main thing was that he was there, near me, and that the light became tinged with satin and silk.

With his arms crossed over his chest, he sat down, as light as a breeze. I always had a cup of coffee or tea for my visitor, which he did not drink. Nor did he touch the snack that I prepared for him. Either he was not hungry or our food was not to his taste, or he did not eat at all any more, through a kind of perpetual fast, as practised by mystics. He listened to me and only seemed to be there for that purpose. And I did not hesitate to chatter away. Most eloquently. Deafening myself. Like people who are really carefree.

I had a greater and greater need to pour my heart out; I let the words carry me on, I forgot to eat, sometimes I stopped working. I laughed a lot too. In bursts. With the stumps of all my teeth sticking out. I did not bother putting my hand in front of my mouth. He did not take offence and did not even seem to notice. He was elegance and good manners personified. Nothing bothered him and nothing amazed him. Had he seen other people like me? Definitely, he had.

One evening when I did not feel so talkative, due to the fever and because I was concentrating on an order to be delivered urgently, he unfolded his arms, like an invitation and raised his eyebrows as though asking a question. I realized then that he wanted to know why I was working so hard.

We needed the money, I told him, a lot of money. Not only in order to feed ourselves but also especially to strengthen the ground-floor doors and windows, block up the garage door which was too easy to open: our father's car and fishing equipment had already vanished.

He fixed his eyes on my skull, staring at my blood-stained, oozing wounds.

'The antibiotics are very expensive; at the moment, we have to provide for immediate demands,' I said.

I finished off the sentence, and my health was not on the agenda. Besides, an abscess had never killed anyone. I came back to the main points.

At the moment, it would cost a fortune to make the outer doors secure. But we definitely had to have this important work done, not just to make them burglar-proof. It was now essential to make the house earthquake-proof, since, I explained, like dust blown on the wind, the news of girls, very young girls alone in a large house passed from mouth to mouth, from ear to ear... The earth shook from the tremors, its bowels were overheated. When it was at boiling point, the noise did not even spare deaf people. In short, a history of geothermic energy that was far from elaborate. I had seen that on TV, I asserted. Then one had to think about the two unfortunate animals, the fish and the bull – I had read that in the Holy Book – who held up our old earth. If these two old animals reached the point of collapse, the whole world would suffer the consequences.

As the fever was at its height, I ended my speech on a note of doubt, that of not making myself clear.

But I heard him responding to me with advice. (He was going to give me more of that; for a long time I would not do anything without his advice.) I could not say with what words, or in what language this advice was given. But I knew that I had to keep the sharp kitchen tools beside me, as well as the garden ones. This would sometimes be an efficient way of frustrating the tremors and these stories of the earth overheating... While waiting for the building work to be finished.

Just as day began to break, he left as usual. I dozed off, exhausted but at peace.

23

We were becoming aware that we attracted attention in the town through the rate of anonymous telephone calls, and the warnings of our neighbours. Our neighbours, the widows, old women or the wretched – in other words, the plebs – who, like us, did not live under authority or the guardianship of someone telling them how to act and behave, forbidding them, among other things, to mix with the fisherman's daughters, the cursed, the depraved, etcetera; these neighbours no longer had any hesitation in knocking on our door.

Some of them were satisfying their curiosity.

'My po-or face, oh what a pit-ity! A gi-girl in the flower of her youth!' Noria cried after they had gone.

A few other women sighed admiringly:

'Upon my word, these little fledglings are managing all right.'

Of course they all wanted to walk religiously on the ground trodden by the one who had dared to break the law, our mother, who was now enjoying the pleasures of love...

Ah, well.

We opened our door to everyone, regardless. Also, they were very useful to us, our inquisitive, greedy neighbours. In exchange for a hot bath, for themselves and their children, fresh vegetables and milk chocolate, they would help the twins with the most difficult chores: the washing, carpet-beating, cleaning the walls with plenty of water, as our mother liked to do.

All the same, we had to keep our distance from some of our bathing-visitors, who tried to worm things out of Noria and Fouzia. Things, in fact, that we had no idea about.

How did our mother go about meeting her lover? At dawn, when our father was sailing on fishy waters? At night, at the time when the red liquor was taking hold of our father? Who helped her? Her messenger? The eldest one, who was an expert in these things? (No secret is impregnable, our father *dixit*.) Did Allouchi send her presents? Did they meet at his place or in a hotel in town? Did he come here? Did they do it under Zeitoun's roof? A real master stroke, this betrayal committed by the orphan girl with velvety eyes brimming with ingenuousness.

Without saying a word, sometimes nodding their

heads, not even picking up the questioners' unpleasant insinuations, Noria and Fouzia listened proudly and with deep interest to what they then thought was an apology for love. It should be said that Amina untiringly used to read to them stories that introduced them to the delights of forbidden liaisons and wild passions.

One woman spoilt everything.

'A holy goody-goody, oh, yes, this Nayla!' she exclaimed as she clicked her tongue. 'Ah! the saucy one ...'

Upon hearing these words, Noria and Fouzia stiffened, but immediately recovered their verbal skills. I caught them drowning the woman in question with insults, then all the others, bluntly, treating them as jealous women and a pack of liars, widows and divorced females; our own Mother could be accused of having two husbands, and maybe even other aspirants, and certainly a list of suitors, nature having been extremely kind to her, whilst they themselves, who were huge *merguez*, giant haggis, had been left out when Allah clothed his creatures with beauty.

'The heartbeats of emotion, I pity you who don't know such things,' Noria chanted while Fouzia showed them out.

'Go on, out you go!' she hissed between her teeth.

From that day on, the two younger ones covered their faces with the veil of solemnity, or that of maturity. For whatever reason, they were very keen on their sister's reading.

Opposite our house, Youssef Allouchi's garden was turning into a dump – as the binmen did not come any more, the residents of the neighbourhood got into the habit of throwing their rubbish in there – and his house, which was ransacked and vandalized, became a shelter for tramps. They would arrive at dusk and disappear at dawn, without anybody knowing who they were. Maybe they were survivors from the earthquake looking for warmth and hospitality. Maybe... If we could at least have seen them. At least to establish that they were human beings... But nobody dared to go near the house, to find out exactly what type of people these hostages to fortune were. Too bad if anyone went hungry: it was certainly no time for being inquisitive. In any case, not about things like that. The whole neighbourhood was a rough sea.

We were restricted to whispers. One question led to another, and ended up with this one: What if they were jinnees?

Definitely, they were jinnees looking for one of their own kind... Oh, yes, the jinnee who had in the past possessed our neighbour, now usurped by the orphan with the velvety eyes, the holy goody–goody!

What if the wronged jinnee was one of them? Of course she was one of them. Did she believe that Allouchi's betrayal, then his disappearance, was the work of those in the neighbourhood? Some sort of plot. So she would keep coming back with her own kind. She would take her revenge. No doubt about that. Maybe they were wrong. How was one to know?

Then it was decided to clean up Youssef Allouchi's garden, to stop messing it up, as rubbish was a chosen haunt of bad jinnees. Everybody joined in the work, women, men and children. The earth was weeded and watered; too bad about the water being used up for this purpose. The furniture and household crockery were brought back.

The Imam, despite having just retired in order to spend his time fishing, went to a great deal of trouble and cleansed the house by numerous incantations, both at dawn and sunset. Seven nights running, candles burned in each corner of the house where the disgraced jinnee had loved, and incense swept away the bad smells. All the time that this was being done, great care was taken not to allow ourselves to be taken by surprise by the mysterious guests. And gradually our neighbour's house regained its past appearance, as if it were inhabited. Even the nightingale came back. Thus it was confirmed that the jinnees, may Allah spare us, may we not die before our time, were indeed the source of these troubles.

At the same time, my wise man's visits became less frequent. I did not make any connection with the peace which now permeated the neighbourhood and took over the house across the road.

That's how the summer ended.

24

As in the time of Aziz the fisherman and his glory, and as
if we had a man in the house, by common agreement,
access to the balcony and the terrace was forbidden; our
shutters stayed shut, and our doorways were now
reinforced. But the anonymous calls went on.

On the advice of my nocturnal visitor, I equipped
myself with a tape recorder. Patiently and persever-
ingly, I watched TV in search of a scene where a man
would say 'Hello.' I managed to record an actor in an
Egyptian film. Each time the phone rang, Professor
Invisible, as we had named his voice, answered with
endless manly 'hellos'. As a result the women who
lived in our neighbourhood, who went on coming to
see us, would casually ask for news of our guest from
the banks of the Nile and, while doubt about our

flighty habits changed into certainty, the telephone calls became less frequent, then they stopped.

Fouzia and Noria used to restrict their outings to shopping in the market, where they went without their former keenness, which had heralded the early stages of our independence. My wounds were not healing. Fever became second nature to me.

The night before they were due to go back to school, Noria announced that she was not going to school.

I was very tired.

'Nor I,' said Fouzia in turn.

Amina clapped.

'Welcome to the club.'

Yasmina did not agree with this. Nor did I.

'We want to write stories,' was Fouzia's announcement.

'Like Ariadne?' Amina asked.

'I d–don't know what school would te-teach us that.'

'The school is in an earthquake zone,' Fouzia groaned.

'You're going to go to school,' I said.

There was no argument about my command; nevertheless I told my counsellor about my sisters' wishes. To my great amazement, he approved of their decision.

I was irritated.

'But what am I going to do about them? Their

future is at stake!'

He muttered some words on free will, a few more on abolishing sinful deeds . . . what was he telling me?

'I can't feed them for their whole life!' I burst out.

The pastel shades in the room faded. Soon not the slightest trace was left. Then I saw my guest in a metallic light. And, as I became angrier and angrier, his white clothes changed colour to darkness.

'But you know as well as I do that they're not even able to write a letter properly,' I went on, more quietly.

He did not utter a word; his eyes shone with disapproval.

'And,' I went on, 'I'm not at all well. Soon I won't be able to see at all. I won't be able to embroider, even to darn a sock.'

A cold wind ruffled my clothes. Once more, I was attacked by fever and this man whom I believed to be a wise man was steering my family's fate towards some unknown disaster.

I tried to explain.

'It may be that Heaven has granted them this gift,' I said, shivering.

'Writing isn't a career, someone once told me.'

No reaction. Only this icy look. But what exactly was he scolding me for?

'What's more, school is compulsory up to the age of fourteen,' I went on. 'And Father would like to have a doctor or an astronaut in the family . . . Noria and Fouzia could still do that.'

At that point, he repeated his arguments about free

will, and lambasted the arbitrary. I refused to fall out with my friend.

As if I were throwing a bottle into the sea, I said: 'In order to write, one has to be educated – at least a little.'

Suddenly it was pitch dark. I staggered towards the kitchen, looking for the emergency switch. Halfway there, the light came on again and my night visitor was no longer there.

Immediately, I knew who he was. He was the jinnee disguised as a wise old man and that was why he had no wrinkles. He had confused me with my mother, because of the patchouli, maybe; this jinnee took me for her rival and she had come to take revenge upon me. When she was unmasked, she vanished. However, I suspected that she would want to come back. In what shape, next time? I had no idea. In any case, I would recognize her and I would not miss her.

I dissolved an aspirin in a bowl of herbal tea. I took little sips of my concoction and started to look for the brazier that our father used for burning his benzoin. I had to purify the house. Right now. Tomorrow I would call the Imam.

The thick smoke from the benzoin was still clinging to the walls when the doorbell rang. It was two o'clock in the morning. I turned a deaf ear. But the shrill ringing started again and did not stop, tearing the silence apart, waking up the twins, who found me sitting on the floor with my legs spread out, looking paralysed with fear, my eyes staring at the embers which were now covered with a thin layer of ash.

'Somebody's ringing the bell,' said Yasmina, her eyes puffy with sleep.

'It's two o'clock in the morning,' I rapped out without moving a hair.

'Who can it be, do you think?' Amina asked.

'It's the jinnee,' I said without batting an eyelid. 'That's why I cleansed the house. We've got to do that every day. Every night. The Imam will recite a few suras. From tomorrow.'

In spite of being worried, the twins looked at each other with some amusement.

'You're not going to set to as well?' Amina asked.

'In any case, you're not going to behave like the neighbours,' Yasmina added.

The bell was ringing furiously.

'Watch from the window and you'll see that I'm right,' I said.

'Oh, no!' Amina shuddered.

The jinnee must not find out how frightened we were. Out of bravado I got up and opened a shutter. Then I saw a man's bald head. With the noise made by opening the window, the ringing died away; the visitor's face could be seen. I drew back. She had returned. Looking like my father. She didn't waste any time.

Yasmina in turn looked out the window.

'It's Father' she shouted.

'It's a trap,' I said.

Keep calm. Above all, don't open the door. Call the Imam straight away. But the twins were already downstairs, shooting the bolts on our strong door one after another. I threw a handful of benzoin powder on to the coal which was still burning, hoping that by doing so, I could get rid of the intruder.

It was no good. As our father would have done, she delighted in fumes. (A pretence, obviously.) Just like our father, she watched us silently, with unspeaking eyes. And in order to dispel any suspicion, she looked at me and asked:

'Who's that?'

'It's your eldest daughter, Father,' my sisters answered.

Then she peered at me with one eye, just as our father used to do after downing a good few bottles. I looked down very submissively. I said nothing. I had to play-act as well. I would play this game a bit better.

'If it's her, she's certainly changed,' my father commented.

Who was not our father.

Then, sitting down, with one leg straight out:

'It can't be her.'

'You've changed too, you've changed a lot,' Amina stated.

In fact she did not have our father's hippopotamus-like shape, nor his fat, flabby cheeks. She had several other manufacturing defects, so to speak, which did not deceive us. Certainly I was not taken in: the wooden leg, the pilgrim's staff, the scars on her face, the burn-marks on the backs of her hands and arms which were not those of our father.

But just as he would have done, she launched into this speech:

'I cannot allow Allouchi's daughters to call me Father, or allow them to speak to me. What's more, you must think about leaving my home. I'm not going to house other people's rejects indefinitely.'

She could not bear her lover's children, who had been borne and brought into the world by another woman. Me, she thought. No doubt about that. All this because of a drop of patchouli.

Then she spoke to me:

'You, stranger, if you want to live under my roof, you will be my ally. If not, out you go!'

She really had a cheek. But I agreed, expecting to be able to fight her by adopting her own tactics; I would make a study of them and would apply them unfailingly.

'Right now, I'm hungry,' she said.

I obeyed.

In the belief that my father was really our father, the twins dragged their feet like victims of torture, quietly weeping.

I heated up the leftovers from supper as I muttered:

'Oh, yes, Ji-ji, whatever you like.'

25

Ji-ji stayed in our parents' room, using their bathroom, the sofa of Aziz the fallen fisherman, of whom we still had no news. She smoked her cigarettes but did not drink wine at all. A big mistake. She wore his clothes. She talked like him, watched TV, jumping from one programme to another, avoiding the news. She insulted the girls just as our father would have done. With her only foot – our real procreator had always had two legs – she turned everything upside-down that she found in her way.

Zanouba, who now wandered around the house on all fours, was kicked so that she was thrown up against the walls and her little body was covered in bruises. In fact, the one-legged visitor was as bad-tempered as sidi Zeitoun. And, from one day to the next, her presence stirred up the household as much as a cavalry regiment. One would have said that we had a man in the house.

There were days when she did not let me out of her sight; more and more, she melted into my shadow, and could not stop taking me into her confidence. (Excellent war strategy.) She told me about her life, getting bogged down in the details, which I had no trouble unravelling, pretending to help her restore her memory. In fact, I made her more entangled. (War tactic.) She dwelt on the confiscated trawlers, which were definitely requisitioned on account of the funny business which was conducted against Aziz the fisherman, set up by Youssef Allouchi and his daughters, the eldest of whom, one Samira (*me!*), had now to make good use of her body, up there, very high up, on the mountain tops.

Then, by innuendo, and indicating the private parts of her body, she talked about castration. Nothing left, she said. *Niet*, my friend. That drew forth a few sobs. *Niet. Niet.* In the end, she was obsessed by it, etc. But what could one do? (That was in the event of our discovering her intimate details, which had to be female.) She collected that kind of distraction, Ji–ji.

On the rare occasions when she talked about our mother, she talked about murder. A premeditated murder. Therefore an assassination. Enough evidence would have to be collected to send them to the scaffold. Oh, yes . . .

In fact, I was her only enemy.

Then she started to send my clients away, on the pretext that they were the special envoys from her well-read neighbour who had come to spy on her. I lost all of them. No more work. No more money. Hello, bankruptcy, but I still had heaven-sent energy. Oh, yes, Ji-ji.

That was how she took over our father's identity and his behaviour in order to set us adrift. And we did go adrift. But we had only lost one battle.

Poverty broke in through our doors and settled in as head of the household. We had only one meal a day, pasta or plain rice; we made our mouths water with imaginary fried sardines or a crust of bread soaked in olive oil. Zanouba and Mahmoud lost their strength and the girls got thin. The neighbours did not come any more, in the first place because they thought our father had come home, second because there was nothing to nibble any more, or anything to swipe. We did not even have any shampoo, as powdered soap had taken its place.

At that point, Khadija reappeared.

It was noon. Fouzia and Noria were at school, preferring that to the thumps and the scenes caused by their so-called father; the twins were having baths; the babies were sleeping; Ji-ji was watching TV, smoking, flicking through the channels, coughing, flicking through the channels, spitting, flicking through the channels.

That day, I was putting water on the fire when the heavy front door banged shut. Then a woman's high heels pounded up the steps of our stairs, echoing and stirring the household. The intruder turned off the TV, and drew herself up, watchful; the babies woke up. Was it a client who did not know about my enforced retirement? I planted myself in the hall, ready to catch her before the other one intervened.

She was wearing a green suit, the skirt well above the knees; she had very short hair and was wearing lipstick to brighten up her mouth, as well as mascara to emphasize her eyelashes.

'If you came because of the advertisement, it's no good,' I said. 'I don't do any more embroidery,' I added.

She brushed me aside with her handbag.

'I'm family,' she said. 'I'm Omar's wife.'

I recognized her tone of voice, then her eyes, then herself. She did not know me at all. Yasmina and Amina came rushing in in their bathrobes. In response to their dumbfounded looks, my sister-in-law dropped her handbag and opened her arms wide, graciously.

She began to thunder:

'*This is me!* Khadija! *Your sister-in-law!* Don't you remember me, *my very dear?*'

Going from one to the other, she shook them, hugged them tight, and covered them with kisses. Then she drew back so as to see them better, to see that she had at last found them, with the moist eyes of someone who has left long ago, and has finally come back. Having done with effusiveness, she said, 'My luggage is down at the bottom of the stairs.' Then she became specific: 'There are presents inside.'

The twins complied. My sister-in-law charged around house; she quickly greeted the person she took for *her father-in-law* and continued on her way down the passage leading to the bedrooms, opening one door after another.

'*Where is my baby? Where is Moud? My little baby? Oh, my love*...My little man...Oh! *you look so moody*...But I'm here now.'

It was indeed Khadija, but she was so different from the person who had covered herself with a veil from head to toe, who never raised her voice, who smiled sparingly, who only spoke in the language of the Holy Book, with supporting quotations. She was radiant, beautiful, happy to see us again. She had a problem accepting who I was, discreetly sympathized with me, just enough to spare me from annoyance, or distress.

'You've got to look after yourself, my poor little girl,' she said.

'Did you not appeal to me to repent, my dear sister-in-law?'

She took my hand, nearly put her lips on it, ready to kiss it. But she drew back, saying:

'Forgive me. Forgive me, I didn't know. Your mother told me all about it.'

'Oh?'

'I'm asking you to forgive me. I am, really.'

'You're forgiven,' I said.

She promised to send me antibiotics, to take me to the United Kingdom to see plastic surgeons . . .

I smiled.

'Send me a wig,' I said.

'Of course. What kind would you like? Fair? Brown? Red? Short? Long? Curly?'

She found her *daddy-in-law* very thin, and he, of course, did not recognize her and ordered her to skedaddle immediately.

'One more sent packing,' Ji–ji grumbled.

In any case, Khadija did not expect to stay for ever.

We were in her apartment, sitting around her, discovering her like a new country. She fed her son and Zanouba with a fruit compote *made in UK*, tickled them all over with Shakespeare's language, then she told us that she had come back to take her baby, take him across the Channel where Omar, Nayla and Youssef Allouchi were waiting for them in a *bed and breakfast*.

She told us everything all at once, without any punctuation, keeping her eyes on Moud who was mumbling, calling one of his aunts 'Mummy'.

The welcoming smiles froze. Then silence fell. Noria and Fouzia started to chew their nails. Amina got up, rather slowly. She straightened herself up like a soldier saluting at the trooping of the colour. Then she took a deep breath and her face was clouded with solemnity. She said:

'That you shorten your skirts, wear make-up, travel alone, is none of our business. On the contrary, we're happy about it. Just as, of course, we applaud our brother's choice. On the other hand, we cannot put up with lies. Religion or no religion.'

Then after a pause, waiting:

'OK, baby?'

'Your mother and her husband are over there. It's a long, very complicated story, but it's the truth,' our sister-in-law said.

Our faces showed very clearly that we needed to know more.

She went on:

'Allouchi nearly had problems about a play that he wrote in the desert. The story was based on the origins of earthquakes, tectonic plates or something like that. Someone had stolen the manuscript. He noticed this the night before the wedding. Obviously that rattled him very badly. He told Omar about it, and Omar advised him to flee. Besides, there was no choice. Your mother followed him willingly. She could never have put up with living in the neighbourhood; she was so ashamed about this business of a second marriage...'

Noria and Fouzia wept. The twins could not utter a word.

'It must be said that Youssef Allouchi is an admirable man,' my sister-in-law added. 'I think they get on well together.'

160

Fouzia blew her nose.

'Have we got other brothers and sisters?' she asked.

'Not at the moment,' Khadija replied. 'I didn't want to tell you straight away, but I'm going to tell you anyway: Allouchi has promised to look after you. As soon as possible.'

'And how?' asked Fouzia.

'By a process which will definitely take some time but in the end...'

'What process?' Amina asked as she clenched her teeth.

'The Crémieux process. What I mean is, the Crémieux decrees had made his mother a French citizen – don't ask me any more about it, it's in the history books. To be truthful, I don't understand a lot about it myself. What you must understand is that, on account of this marriage with your mother, you will all be French, we will all be French, and that's how you will be able to join them. If that's what you want, of course.'

'But what are you doing in England if Crémieux is a Frenchman?' Fouzia asked.

'Because the *bed and breakfasts* are offered to us free. Also, it's an EEC story. [She pronounced it "eece".] And it's temporary.'

'What kind of a story?'

'EEC...I don't know how to explain it very well. Just accept that it's going to work out all right for everyone. OK?'

'And Father?' asked Noria.

'Who's a sick man,' Fouzia joined in.

161

'We can't leave him alone here,' said Amina. 'I'm the one who'll stay with him,' she added.

'We know why,' said Fouzia, teasingly.

'Because Father's a human being and he's our father,' Amina cut in.

'And be–because your lover wouldn't be entitled to Crémieux,' said Noria.

'Father isn't our father,' I mumbled.

'He really is sick,' Amina added.

'You'll decide when the time comes,' said Khadija. Then she fell upon her suitcases.

'And now, the presents! Your mother and Allouchi have sent them to you.'

I looked at my sister-in-law. She was not a bit like the friend that she had been before she became part of our family. Suddenly I wondered whether Khadija was indeed Khadija.

'Besides, one doesn't know who's who any more,' I mumbled.

She spent two days packing her bags. On the black market, she exchanged a few pounds for a wad of dinars. She did a great deal of shopping, cooked a full couscous and tagines with olives and prunes, soups of every colour for us and passed on some clothes and make-up.

'Girls, you must make yourselves pretty. Go out, face the earthquakes and volcanoes. Life is too short,' she said as she hastily scribbled the address of the bed and breakfast.

She went off with her baby, whom we will miss, the twins sniffed. She promised to give our love to our mother, our brother and our father-in-law. Of course, she insisted that we should endure our miseries. It would help our mother's husband speed up the process. They would write to us and all that.

'*See you soon, my dearest*. See you very soon.'

Fouzia gave her a parcel.

'These are presents for Mother,' she said.

Noria wiped away a tear.

'Patchouli and thi-ings.'

'See you soon.'

'Very soon.'

'S-soon, very s-soon, Go-od willing...'

For a few days, in accordance with the twins' decision, Khadija's visit was a taboo subject. They refused to latch on to hopes that would turn into delusions. But they continued to write constantly and watched out for the postman. Who, having recently been snowed under, hardly ever called. As for me, I was filled with remorse: what were we to say to the prudish veiled Khadija, the real Khadija, when she came back to collect her son ?

I would see to that when the time came. Just now, we had to banish from within our walls the jinnee who had passed herself off as Aziz Zeitoun. Who was not giving up. Who wanted my skin.

And we were hungry.

26

I watched her. She pretended not to notice, and put this down to my devotion. She took advantage of my docility and was pleased with it. I helped her to dress, to have a bath; just like her arms, her hands and her face, the rest of her body was scored with scars. And then this large stump at the beginning of the thigh. How could she have had this abominable amputation done to her? Oh, yes, she came from a world where love was worth every kind of mutilation. I dressed her and shaved her. With her eyes shut, and half-asleep, she held out the skin on her neck, her throat and her carotid artery in reach of the razor. She defied me. She tested me. But that was not my style, not true to our family. . . I would go about things differently in order to get rid of you, Ji-ji, yes, to get rid of you and send

. you back where you belong. For ever.

When I had finished sprinkling eau-de-Cologne over her and patted her cheeks with a hot towel which she loved, she kissed me on my forehead, then kissed me on the back of my hand and mumbled countless thank-yous, praised her ancestors and blessed my own. She was worried about my health, asked me several times a day about what dreadful thing had happened to my poor head. An accident, I answered, laconically.

Then she repeated, staring at her wooden leg:

'Oh ! Accidents . . . That's me, nothing else happens, just accidents. And I have come back from a faraway place, believe me.'

In fact, my lack of appetite, there being nothing much to eat, seemed to bother her too . . .

'You've got to eat well if you want to fight this Armada with me,' she said.

Then, as she took my measure:

'You're really thin . . . It's because you've got no teeth that you don't eat. Was that an accident as well ?'

'I-it wa-as an ac-cident too . . .'

Just like the real impostor wise man, she did not eat, or only a little, just enough to dispel any doubts. But from morning to night she was exhausted, she stubbornly stated that she belonged to the Zeitoun family, she was very proud of this, called upon her dead pious grandfather, his generosity, his sense of honour, the fortune which he made by the sweat of his brow, his charitable gifts to the poor . . . Then returning to the fall from grace of Aziz Zeitoun, to treason and his plans for revenge.

'I don't know who you are, or who sent you,' she told me. 'But without you, those women would already have torn me to shreds. As soon as I'm better, you'll help me, won't you?'

I nodded in agreement.

Now that she was pacified, with a faraway look, as if I were no longer there, she went on:

'My ancestors sent you to save me from their claws and save my honour... Their honour.'

Then she started to laugh like a madwoman.

'Between ourselves, there is nothing left to save, as regards honour,' she said looking down at the flies of our father's trousers.

Then, no longer laughing, she looked at me:

'Let's save our lives, that's what matters now...'

One day, while I was concocting our supper out of the leftovers from the cooking done by the woman in the short skirts, she shouted:

'My aunt!'

She dropped her pilgrim's staff and limping rushed towards me.

'I've just noticed that it's you! Oh my dear aunt! How happy I am to see you again!'

Then she threw herself on my neck and wet it with her tears. That lasted for ever. The twins were rather touched by this.

'He's completely lost his reason,' said Amina.

'Something must be done,' Yasmina replied.

'Father's not Father!' I shouted at them.

'But that's what we're saying,' Yasmina said. 'Father isn't Father any more.'

She was really vehement. How could I convince my sisters? I had no rational explanation to give them. I should have introduced them to the impostor old wise man; in the belief that I was doing the right thing, I had not even mentioned him to them. Too bad. She was vehement and I did not insist. However, I had to discuss it all with somebody. I could not pull it off on my own. I needed some back-up. The Imam had sworn never to cross the threshold of our home and of course refused to perjure himself. Santa Cruz! I would go to Santa Cruz. The priest himself would come.

'We've definitely got to do something,' said Amina.

'But what?' I asked.

Then:

'Apart from hospital, I don't know what else.'

'Well, we're not going to lock him up,' said Yasmina. 'After all he's gone through!'

'In any case, she would escape,' I mumbled.

Yasmina opened her eyes really wide.

'What did you say?'

'I said you're right.'

What was the point? I went on:

'If the Imam...'

'The Imam? Father will send him packing straight away,' Yasmina exclaimed.

'And the priest. The priest from Santa Cruz?' I said.

'Are you mad or something? Do you want to see your priest torn to shreds? Also, I think he vanished in an earthquake.'

'I think I know what to do,' Amina interrupted.

'We're listening,' I said.

'My friend, don't you know. . .'

'I don't know anything,' I interrupted.

'Well, you all know that I've got a boyfriend!'

Now she was involving me in her dissolute way of life. I was beside myself.

'Don't tell me that he's going to carry you off, that you're going to play the beauty, like the story of Beauty and some prince or other!'

Amina sighed and looked at Yasmina for help.

'She has a boyfriend and it's not the end of the world,' the latter stated calmly.

'But do you ever think about the effects of what you do?'

'It's not as if you're our mother,' Amina let slip.

I was shaking from head to toe. Sweat was pouring off me. But my voice was as loud as a loudspeaker.

'Who told you that I'm not? Who told you that I didn't give birth to you, just as I did to Zanouba? That you weren't conceived in the shadow of a fiery volcano? In the holes of an earthquake?'

When I had stopped agonizing, I turned on my heel and went into my room.

Behind my back, Amina said in a broken voice:

'Oh, my God, I hope it's just meant to be funny.'

'It's not funny,' Yasmina retorted. 'It's fantasy.'

They were hot on my heels.

'We know what you've been through and what you're still going through,' Yasmina began.

'We're going to look after you and Father,' Amina went on.

'We'll get a doctor to come.'

'That's it,' I said.

I slipped into bed. I needed to think about this and to find an ally. My sisters were far too naïve.

'We're going to look after you,' Yasmina said once more, as she tucked me in.

'Those antibiotics. How are you going to pay for them?' I asked.

Then, with the blankets up to my chin:

'I must always think about everything.'

'We thought about that,' said Yasmina.

Until it was proved otherwise, I was the head of the family.

'Are you going to remove the reinforcing from our doors? Return your expensive purchases? Those canvases, paintbrushes, pencils and tubes of paint?'

'No,' said Yasmina.

'What are the little Van Goghs going to improvise for us? Have they found rich patrons worthy of their works?'

I started to laugh, almost like the Ji-ji.

'Could you calm down a bit,' Yasmina pleaded.

'You're the one who needs to calm down,' I said.

I stopped laughing.

'I know someone,' said Amina.

'I know,' I said resignedly. 'The one you're going to run off with.'

Yasmina's voice suddenly took on a tone of authority:

'She just knows someone whose sister works in the main chemist's shop. We'll talk to him and his sister will give us a kind of credit,' she said all at once.

I stared at Amina with one eye.

'You're preaching venality,' I said with deep sadness. 'I thought you were a romantic.'

'I'm going to make herbal tea,' said Amina.

I sank down under the blankets and mumbled:

'I'd like a brazier and some benzoin, and an Imam. Otherwise, a priest, or a rabbi, anyone stronger than Ji-ji . . . I mean than your father.'

Amina went out backwards. Yasmina nodded. I fell asleep.

27

Someone comes into my room. My eyes are shut but
the steps are those of a man. The twins are with him.
The whisperings reach me like something from a cave.

'The fever doesn't stop any more. More ... more ...'

'She's delirious' ... ous ... ous ...

'She talks to herself' ... self ... self ...

'Sometimes as if she were talking to someone' ...
one ... one ...

Etcetera ... ra ... ra ... ra ...

'She calls our father Ji–ji ...'

JINNEE! JINNEE! JINNEE!

'She doesn't trust him ...'

Ji ... Ji ...

'Quite normal, after what he did to her ...'

ACCIDENT! ACCIDENT!

They stop whispering. They are not talking at all now. My blankets are lifted up. I am turned over on to my side. My bottom is revealed. Then my buttocks are separated. A thin, cold object is placed inside my anus. I think of the time when I was a student nurse. A few moments later, the thin hot object is taken out.

The whispering starts up again.

'That's some temperature'... ure ... ure ...

Then a needle is inserted into my left buttock, or the right, I cannot say which one. They cover me up again. I've still got my eyes shut but then I sleep.

I do not get up any more; I am not strong enough as the antibiotics make my body very tired and now there are scabs all over my wounds. I keep a watchful eye on the intruder. Besides, she makes it easy for me, the silly woman: she comes to see me every day.

She keeps calling me: Oh, my dear aunt.

'Oh, my dear aunt! You're not going to do the same thing as last time,' she says every time she comes. 'You're going to get better. You'll soon get up. Look after me.'

Indeed, I am going to get back to health to look after you, my Ji–ji.

'I need you more than ever,' she goes on. 'More than ever.'

She holds forth. She swears. She commits perjury. She renounces her sins. She confides in me. She foams at the mouth. She harks back to the past. She gets tongue-tied. Her tongue is loosened. Then she starts off on her sermons again. Then she utters oaths. She says the same thing over and over again. She tries to overwhelm me.

My eyes turn towards her, taking in her scarred face, then looking down at the blemishes on her arms like so many tracks furrowing its copious black hair. The stigmata on her hands, her wooden leg, her scarred cheeks: all the manufacturing defects are there, and she continues to claim to be my nephew, Aziz Zeitoun.

'There you are, my dear aunt,' she says. 'I know it's not the time to talk about that, because of your health, but you must know this, so that at least you can get used to the idea.'

She adjusts her wooden leg. She clears her throat. She fiddles with her moustache, then she scratches it hard. She looks at me sideways. She talks in a teenager's voice.

She says:

'I'll have to get married again.'

She stops at nothing to bewilder me. But I keep thinking clearly. I smile feebly. That reassures her.

'Don't you see, my dear aunt,' she goes on. 'Now I'm a widower. A ruined widower. Robbed. Betrayed. Of course, you know all that . . .'

She weeps. She sobs. She gasps. She snivels. She blows her nose. She wipes away her tears.

Solemnly, she says:

'I'm putting you, my dear aunt, in charge of finding a fiancée for me. I'd like to have a woman to give me a helping hand, to get my dignity back. Your decision will be mine, my dear aunt. An old, ugly woman or an invalid, whoever you choose, I'll take her. I swear it. On your grave, my dear aunt.'

She gives herself away there, but straight away she corrects herself:

'I mean, on your life, my dear aunt.'

But she is worried. Maybe I have unmasked her, once more, like when she turned up in the guise of a wise man. I do not rise.

She says, evasively:

'Also, I'll never have any more children. They took away my equipment...'

I feel she is about to burst out laughing but my stern look makes her change her mind.

She says:

'My dear aunt, would you like to inhale a little benzoin?'

I nod in agreement.

She turns her head towards the door. She tries to shout but her voice is weak.

'The brazier and some benzoin. Make it sharp-ish!'

She coughs and spits into her handkerchief.

'The same doctor looks after us,' she begins again. 'If it's our ancestors' wish, we will get better on the same day... And they will want that for us; they are favourably disposed to me at the moment. They no longer have any reason to have it in for me, no pretext for ignoring me and even less for hurting me. Don't you see, my dear aunt, maybe you could see it yourself, that I never drink a drop of wine any more, I have lost the taste for it. Can you imagine it, my dear aunt? Weaned. That's all I've gained. Anyway, as the mouse said after pissing in the sea, it's one more drop in the ocean.'

She lets out a giggle. She goes on:

'We'll get better. As you know, my dear aunt, I have faith in doctors. Last time, if you had taken my advice, if you had accepted that operation, you would not have gone away and nothing that has happened would have happened at all . . . Oh, but on that subject, would you have given in in the end? Would you have had your gall-bladder removed? Is that why you are back home?'

She really takes me for a half-wit. Otherwise, she is trying to make me crack up. I steal a glance at her: The blame is always on me, Ji-ji, and my gall-bladder is inside me, producing bile. It will go on producing it as long as you hang around my family.

'That's all water under the bridge,' she goes on. 'Now, it's about going forward. Only, you've got to watch out for yourself, my dear aunt. Don't trust Allouchi's daughters. They act like nice obedient girls and all that. But don't trust them, in particular you mustn't talk to them about my imminent remarriage. That's because soon these bastards will show themselves in their true colours. Although, Allah be praised, you know, the most dangerous one, the ringleader who sleeps anywhere, with anyone, is gone.'

The smoking brazier appears. She gets up. I look suspicious. In spite of myself. And she sees it. Then she winks at me behind Yasmina's back.

She says:

'You know how much I like benzoin, but I need to rest for a while. I'll let you think about the plan you know about.'

I mumble:

'Of course, apple of my brother's eye.'

She limps over to the door, her wooden leg knocks on the tiles in the passage, blotting out the sobbing of the twins, who were swallowed up in the white smoke.

28

At last scars formed; they were ugly, of course, but irrefutable evidence that I was getting better. No more fever, no more nightmares... The man who gave me injections in my bottom stopped coming. There was another one who came instead of him, but this fellow spaced out his visits. He talked a bit more than the last one; he asked questions about everything; he wanted to know my dreams, my fears as well as my desires... He thought he was Freud or the most popular marabout in the area. I answered him in a matter-of-fact way, often with my mind a thousand leagues away. Sometimes I felt a need to tell him about the intruder, and her Machiavellian plans. However I did nothing about it: I needed an Imam and some benzoin, not the pink and white pills that I swallowed under his indulgent eye. I was still considered to be ill and I wanted him to believe it.

I could get up, walk over to the window and I could leave my bedroom, the house, the town, the country or the continent and go far, far away, to the north, where it is black and white, and live with the wolves. But I did not want her to know that I was really well. And she too, went on limping and getting thinner, and her visits were becoming rarer. In fact, she was acting like an invalid. We used the same tricks, even in hate, as closeness creates likenesses. But unlike me, who always kept my perspicacity, sometimes she forgot things and gave herself away. Being unable to resist remembering her femininity, she would wear one of my mother's dresses, close-shave her moustache, go all over the house and settle down on the terrace. She howled about the loss of her virility, her honour that had been trampled on, how our grandfather was turning in his grave... Then the doctor would give her an injection and she would go back to bed.

From dawn onwards, I sit in front of a window. My eyes look for the sea shimmering with the morning light but they do not see it any more. Or very little. I can only see a scrap of blue escaping from between the buildings which are being erected all the time. Having recently been sold, the little house across the road has been transformed into a large building. So much for the blue of the sea; the heavenly blue is left.

For some hours, I fill my time with the movement in the street and I listen to its rumbles, to which I cling as if it were a swan-song. Children stamping on a balloon, their shindy dying away at dusk, the shutters banging shut at the same time. Then the silence which holds the street in its grip. Then the night which stirs up the rumbles of the earth and the shouting of women and children. Then the silence of the nightingale. Sleep cold-shoulders me, I ask for it but it becomes stubborn and deserts me. Then Yasmina and Amina read to me. Yasmina reads letters, Amina reads books. I cannot take anything in. That's how I go to sleep.

This morning, some post came. I saw the postman with his postbag which bounced on his hip and a large yellow parcel under his arm. Then I heard him ring the bell. Then shouts of joy raised the earth.

A moment later, the twins rush into my bedroom. Yasmina is carrying the parcel. She sets it down on my desk. She quivers with delight. She points to it. It is covered with a few red stamps; it is firmly tied with string.

'A parcel from Mother!' she yelps.

'Open it,' says Amina.

'We're waiting for Fouzia and Noria,' says Yasmina, calming down.

Amina clenches her fists. She is stamping her feet.

'Open it,' she pleads.

She is exasperating me.

Yasmina shows great self-control.

'More than a few hours,' she mumbles.

And supposing it is a booby-trapped parcel?

'Leave this parcel where it is, and get out of here,' I say abruptly. 'Go on, into the garden, as far as possible. Don't forget about Zanouba.'

Yasmina nods her head. She is weary.

'I'm the one who is going to open this parcel,' I say.

Then I explain:

'It must be booby-trapped.'

'It can't be booby-trapped,' Yasmina retorted. 'It's from Mother.'

Yasmina's expression shows clearly what she thinks of me.

'I'm not mad.'

Outside, a car slams on its brakes in a screeching of tyres. Then a child starts to cry.

'This parcel can't be booby-trapped,' Yasmina insists.

'We can never be too careful,' I mumbled.

'If it's really booby-trapped, you'll go with it,' says Amina.

I shout at her:

'It's nothing to do with you!'

'And the postal orders are booby-trapped, too?' Amina shouts in turn.

'What postal orders?'

'The postal orders which feed us and pay for the medicines and doctors.'

'I don't know a thing about what's going on.'

Women run into the street. They plead to Heaven. Then a murmur reveals that they are thanking Him, praising Him. The child is safe.

Without saying a word, Amina opens the drawer of my desk. She takes out a pair of scissors. She cuts the string. Yasmina lets her do it. I close my eyes. There is not a sound. Even the street is drowned in fleeting silence. I take a deep breath.

'There's a wig for you,' says Amina.

I breathe out. I open my eyes. I see a mop of red hair sticking out of its box.

'Would you like to try it on?' Yasmina asks.

'I don't want it,' I say. 'It must surely be made of poodle-hair. It smells like a dog, too.'

Then:

'Who sends us postal orders?'

'Mother and Allouchi, don't you see!'

'Instead of the Crémieux decrees?'

'In one of the letters, they said that it's going to happen soon,' Amina says as she rummages inside the parcel.

'When?'

'They don't say exactly when.'

'I knew that this woman was telling us a lot of poppycock.'

I pretend to yawn. My sisters leave my room. They do not forget the parcel.

I do not see her any more, nor hear her voice or her

uneven footsteps on the tiles. I lie in wait for her arrival. In vain. The man who asks questions comes less and less often. It's Yasmina now who gives me the pink and white pills, sometimes other capsules. Nobody talks about her. I ask no questions. Maybe she is not here any more? Has she finally given up the struggle and gone back to her own people? Maybe that is why Fouzia and Noria are not going to school. The last few days, they are the ones who bring my meals. I feel the twins are very busy. With what? They say nothing.

'Is it holiday time now or is someone starting out on her little career as a novelist ?' I asked, to win their trust.

Noria and Fouzia shake their heads frantically. They have red eyes.

'So are you sick, then? Flu?'

'No, it's Father who's very sick. He doesn't get up at all, any more. He has difficulty in breathing. There are lots of worms coming out of his flesh.'

'The doctor calls th-that bedsores.'

The wallpaper in my bedroom starts curling up; it fades; the flowers are nothing but shapeless stains; I find the curtains hanging at my windows are revolting too. I shall replace them with new ones that I shall embroider myself: they will be in blue velvet decorated with gold and silver thread. I shall take the paper off the walls and paint them ivory white.

Fouzia holds back a tear.

'Bedsores,' she says.

'What did you say?'

They do not answer me. They rub their eyes and sniffle slightly. In a strange way, I do not take pleasure in this first step towards victory. I shall have to wait a bit.

'Are you crying?'

'No...'

'That means you're upset.'

I do not want them to be upset. I do not want my family to suffer. It has already had its share of suffering. Enough!

'You mustn't.'

Then they really burst into tears. It will make them feel better if I tell them the truth. Too bad if they are only children. Besides, I find they are maturing very fast. And stories about genies, especially bad ones, are not unknown to them.

'I'm going to tell you a secret.'

Then:

'If you accept my terms.'

They stop crying.

'All right?'

They agree. But the promise of a secret seems to leave them indifferent. Do they think that I will not tell them? Or do they dread the terms? I wait for some sign of impatience, which does not come. Today, the soup is really good. I swallow the last spoonful and scrape the bottom of the dish.

'Who made the soup?' I ask.

'The twins,' says Fouzia.

'It's really good.'

They agree mechanically. I try to stir up their curiosity.

'Close the door,' I say.

Noria gets up with a tired movement. She shuts the door with a sigh. Just like a grown-up.

'First of all, the terms,' I announce.

Then:

'You must go and find the Imam. If he refuses, you must go to Santa Cruz and ask for the priest. He will not refuse you. He must come immediately to carry out an exorcism. Like in the film. OK?'

'OK.'

'You give me your word?'

'Oh, yes,' they say.

'Now here's the secret.'

I blurt out:

'Father isn't Father.'

I tell them everything: the visits from the impostor wise man, his sudden disappearance followed immediately by the arrival of the person with one leg, his confidences, the so-called emasculation. Khadija who is not Khadija. Everything. Even women-men . . .

They listen to me without complaint. I do not succeed in cheering them up, but my story does not seem to take them by surprise: they believe me. I breath a sigh of relief: they will keep their word.

I repeat:

'The Imam or the priest will make her disappear for good, in view of the fact that she has started to decompose. Otherwise, she will come back in another disguise and will do the same things to us again.'

I add:

'Genies are like the sphinx. Never forget that.'

Yasmina comes in with a glass of water and the pills. I congratulate her on the soup. She holds out the glass for me, then the pills. Before I swallow them, I snatch a look at Noria.

My sisters have kept their promise. They made not only the Imam come but, I think, the whole town: two days later, the house was swarming with people. My room was full of women and children. The women looked at me, sadly nodding, the children were dumbfounded. The twins sent them away. They did not want me to be disturbed. These women did not bother me. On the contrary, I saw future clients in them. But I did not protest. I was waiting for everything to be finished before I announced I was healed.

For dinner, there was a lamb couscous. The men recited prayers until dawn. The telephone never stopped ringing. Next day, I did not leave the window. On the stroke of noon, a man and a woman came into my room. They had puffy eyes, as if they were suffering from a great lack of sleep.

'Come and say goodbye to your father,' the woman said to me.

The man was my mother's brother. I recognized him in spite of his very rare visits to us, a long time ago, when he still lived in the town. He had an ugly wife. I looked away. I stared at the road, waiting for the street-vendor to appear.

'Let us leave her,' said my uncle.

One hour later, I saw the funeral procession. The black crowd of people hid the scrap of blue sky, then it turned a corner. The muezzin's chanting rose into the air. The sun was at its highest. In floods of tears, I thanked God. It was a very long time since I had cried.

29

Next Thursday will be the beginning of spring. Then I shall leave my room. For now, I am getting ready. I must begin everything again, from the beginning: draft an advertisement, send it to the paper; get in touch with my clients again. Buy a tambour frame, as I cannot find my own. I shall not forget to change my curtains and get my walls painted. And, as soon as the money comes in, I shall change the whole house. To my own taste. Too bad if my father and mother do not like it. They would only need to be here. Besides, we still have no news. Of course the neighbours think that our father was at the head of the funeral procession. The neighbours can think what they like, provided that they leave us in peace.

This morning, Yasmina stayed in my room for quite a while. She watched me writing out the advertisement, reading it back, crumple it into a ball, then throw it in the wastepaper basket.

'Do you want me to help you?'

'No, no,' I say. 'It's all right.'

'You dictate and I'll do the writing.'

I shout at her:

'No!'

I start again, but I have no more inspiration. I give up. I shiver slightly. It is cold. Spring is late in coming. I become irritated. I am forgetting something. But what? I am going round in circles. I shut the window to keep the street noises out. I pull the curtains. Yasmina irritates me by watching me doing this. She gets on my nerves even more when she holds out the pink and white pills to me, with the glass of water. I swallow the lot.

But I say:

'All the same, you know that I'm well.'

'I know.'

'How many times do I have to tell you?'

'It's just that you've got to finish the treatment,' she says. 'Those are the Imam's instructions,' she adds.

OK. As it is the Imam. Maybe I'll need that man. One never knows. Anyway, let's touch wood. My table is made of Formica. My bed is made of wrought iron. My wardrobe is wooden, but it is rather old and full of woodworm. I must get rid of all this stuff. I ward off ill fortune by spitting into my bosom. In the good old habit of our country.

I go back to bed. Yasmina does not leave. I lie on my side, turning my back on her. But she stays there. I feel she wants to tell me something that will annoy me. I shiver.

'I'm cold.'

Yasmina is wearing a T-shirt and a short skirt. She puts a blanket over my legs.

'Close the window,' I say.

The window is shut, but Yasmina pretends to close it. She is definitely going to tell me something unpleasant.

She says:

'Are you asleep?'

Here we go.

'We have been summoned to the French Embassy,' she blurts out.

I sit up straight.

'What have we done?'

'We've done nothing at all. We're summoned to collect our passports.'

Amina comes in. She has a box in her hands. She opens it and takes out the wig made of dog's hair.

She smiles.

'We have to appear with photos and birth certificates.'

'I've got my passport already,' I say.

Then Fouzia arrives, with a freshly ironed dress over her arm. Noria proudly presents a pair of carefully polished shoes.

Then as though crying 'Surprise!' with one voice, they exclaim:

'Crémieux!'

They deafen me and I cover my ears with the palms of my hands. The uproar stops. Then I fold my arms. I look at my sisters. They are only children; their credulity, these hopes, this joy, all of this hurts me and tears me apart.

'I'm sick of Crémieux,' I say at last. 'I want to embroider, earn money, fix up the house and look after you. Just like before.'

'But we'll come back,' says Amina.

'I kno-ow that she's promised he-her fian-cé,' says Noria.

'What did the Imam say?' I ask.

'That he's going to marry them as soon as possible,' says Fouzia.

I cast them a withering look.

I ask them:

'What did the Imam say about Crémieux?'

Yasmina gives a little cough.

'He says we should go . . . That girls alone in a big house . . .'

'Well, does he know about Professor Invisible, the voice that says hello? Didn't that work all right? And who precisely is going to look after the house?'

'We've got good security now.'

'Who's going to welcome Father home?'

They cannot find any answer to that one.

'I've always got to think of everything,' I say before

going back to sleep.

Spring is here. Even if it's autumn now. I see it in the leaves on the trees, constantly turning yellow. Just like in the books where the seasons are marked by colours and lights.

My bedroom walls are white. Bright white. I wanted them to be ivory white. However, it's done. I have not finished embroidering the blue velvet curtains. I must say that it takes time and an embroidery project of that size is very demanding. In any case, these curtains will not fit my really high, narrow window. Also, there are bars on it. Why did they put the bars on? I protested. Why do we have bars when the volcanoes are not roaring any more? When the earth does not open any more?

Decidedly these workers, who will end up ruining me, understand nothing. Suddenly, I cannot look out at the road any more. I cannot hear children shouting, the street-vendor, or the call of the muezzin, any more. I can only hear the wind moaning when night falls.

In the daytime all is silent. This helps me to think. I think a lot as I look at a scrap of sky, while waiting for people to answer my advertisement. I shall have to compose another one.

My sisters have engaged a woman to look after me. They have to pay her with the so-called postal orders sent by our mother and her husband. I do not believe one word of it. I suspect that Amina is kept by her fiancé. I am sure that we are once more the subject of slander in the neighbourhood.

The woman who looks after me is fine: she is discreet, she smiles, just what one needs, she is clean and always wears white, but does not talk much or only in French. What's more, she looks like the women on the TV.

My sisters and my daughter do not come into my room quite so often. They have realized that I am dissipated by their presence, that I cannot even write a wretched advertisement properly any more. I lose my appetite and stop talking. The anguish of being unable to start up my own business again is choking me.

One day they pushed open my door, bringing strangers in. Two women and two men. I am never very happy to see strangers. I do not trust them, nor should I ever have done so. I looked away, as a sign of protest, and, all the time that they were under our roof, I stared at the wall or a patch of blue that appeared in the greenery. Then my sisters began to say anything that came into their heads and started telling lies. A new and really annoying habit. A few days ago, they told me that a baby had been born in our home. I had to roar at them to make them confess that they were lying.

Ah, well.

Then they made out one of the women was our mother and the other our sister-in-law, one of the men was my mother's husband and the second Omar. Our so-called mother wore tight-fitting jeans, a low-cut white blouse and high heels. Her face was uncovered and she was flawlessly made up. She did not smell of patchouli. She smelt of something good but very different. Let her thereby disguise herself, let her change her perfume, and be at ease with both men...

Ah, well, let us pray.

But may our mother, Nayla Zeitoun or Allouchi, whatever she is is called nowadays, may our mother now bask in the glow of tenderness, words of affection, and interest in her voice and eyes...Our mother who was taught by no one to use the movements and language of love...I don't know about you, but I have a feeling myself that people take me for a mug.

Sidi Bou Saïd,
Wiepersdorf,
Zurich.